For Gráinne, Éile and Maebh

1

'It's like we're lying in a giant green frying pan,' Rory said.

We were on the grassy slope behind one of the goal-posts on the bowl-shaped football pitch. I was wearing my short-sleeved Ireland jersey with 'Kev' on the back and Rory wore his favourite red T-shirt, the one with the long black sleeves. He had my football under his head as a pillow and I sat next to him, putting on my goalie gloves.

'Did you know,' I said, 'if you put a frog into a pan of hot water, it'll jump out immediately. But if you put him into a pan of cold water and heat the water slowly, then he'll just sit in it and boil to death.'

'How do you know that?' said Rory.

'Sully said so, in the community centre last week when he was frying sausages.'

'Sully is a gas man,' Rory said, laughing.

'Yeah,' I said, gazing up at a straight rope of white smoke that a jet was dragging across the blue sky.

A bee buzzed by Rory's head. 'Feck off, bee,' he said, waving it away.

It was then we heard the squeal of brakes and the noise of a car bumping a footpath. Both of us jumped up. A car roared down the grassy slope at the other end of the pitch and spewed up dust as it shot through the goalposts.

'It's Adam!' Rory cried, as if I didn't already know.

And Madser and Lunchbox were with him. Who else?

'He ... he sees us?!' Rory croaked.

'Yeah, he sees us. He's just showing off. And whatever you do, don't run.'

The car seemed to speed up as it headed directly towards where we were standing, so we backed away from the goal.

I could see Adam's head behind the wheel, his black fringe slicked back and the shades perched on his nose. Lunchbox, the eejit, had his fat bare arse sticking out the back window. Then Adam stuck his head out the driver's door and pointed a finger to let me know that he'd spotted us.

But he must have had trouble doing two things together, pointing and driving, cos the car lurched suddenly to one side and crashed into one of the goalposts, bending it sideways and causing the crossbar to come crashing down.

Lunchbox dropped backwards from the car like he was making a parachute jump. The car's engine spluttered and died and all went quiet for a second or two – except for the loud moans coming from Lunchbox who was lying flat on the ground, belly to the sky, his fat hands groping for the waistband of his tracksuit. Me and Rory didn't move. We just waited and watched.

Madser staggered from the passenger seat with a hand to his bleeding scalp while Adam, inventing a whole new stream of curses, punched the airbag and tried to free himself from the seat belt.

'Hey, Adam,' Madser said, laughing, 'look at the state of Lunchbox!'

Adam jumped from the car and kicked the door shut, then examined the broken sunglasses in his hand and cursed some more before flinging them away. Then he turned towards me. He had that mean, glassy look in his eyes that meant he'd been taking stronger stuff than just his usual cans.

'You'd better not be laughing at me, Short Arse.'

'I'm laughing at Lunchbox,' I yelled.

Madser was prodding at Lunchbox's jelly belly with the tip of his runner like you'd prod at something on the beach to see if it was still alive.

'Dumbo, I told you to wear your seat belt!'

'I think he was wearing it ... before he broke it,' Adam said.

The two of them laughed like hyenas. They looked like hyenas too the way they were circling Lunchbox.

While they were teasing Lunchbox like that, me and Rory went over to inspect the car. It was a silver Volkswagen Golf just a year old. Pasted on the back inside window was a sticker edged with bright red and orange flames that said 'Red Devils For Ever'.

I clicked open the boot and was about to peer in when Adam's rough hand grabbed me by the shoulder.

'Whatya think you're doin', Short Arse?'

'I'm just having a look. OK?'

'It's not OK. It's my car. So get lost!'

'I thought you promised Ma you wouldn't do this crap any more.'

'Why don't you run home to her so? Short Arse!'

I kicked out at Adam's leg, but he batted my kick away and sniggered.

'Ah – little mammy's boy doesn't like his name.'

'Hey, Adam,' Rory called.

Adam turned and stared at Rory like he'd forgotten there were two of us. 'It's your Kev's birthday today.'

'It's your birthday?' he said, turning to me, his eyes crazy blinking like he'd been woken from a spell.

'Yeah. I'm fourteen.'

'Hey! I don't feel too good!' Lunchbox cried, clinging onto the base of the goalpost like he was lost at sea.

'Serves you right for sticking your fat arse out the window,' Adam said.

'He had to stick it out cos he was stinking up the car,' sneered Madser.

They both laughed once more like they were hilarious, then Adam moved to the boot and peered in.

'It's all football crap,' he complained and pulled a pile of neatly stacked red cones out and flung them aside. Next he pulled out a black plastic binbag and emptied it onto the grass. Football training bibs spilled out and he kicked them apart so they scattered in all directions. He rooted once more and found a kitbag. He unzipped it quickly, poked at it, then flung the bag on the ground beside where I was standing.

'Football crap. All useless football crap.'

He took out two corner flagpoles and chucked them too close to the shaking Lunchbox. Then he found a large plastic box and he ripped off the lid. The box was full of files like you'd get in a school office. Adam threw them over his shoulder, letting the papers go wherever the breeze blew them. Madser was rooting around over beside him and found a pair of binoculars. He held them up to his eyes.

'Hey. Where's everything gone?' he cried.

'You're looking through the wrong end, ya dozy eejit.' Adam grabbed them.

'Hey! They're mine, Adam.'

'Who got the best stuff the last time? You did! Now it's my turn. OK?'

Adam didn't wait for Madser to agree. 'Come on,' he said. 'Let's get outta here.'

They turned and, putting their hoods up, walked off.

'What about me?' Lunchbox shouted after them. 'What about me?' He groaned and took one of the flagpoles and, using it like a crutch, got himself to his feet and followed them.

Rory was over at the back of the car gathering together the files and turning pages. 'Look, Kev, this is all to do with money stuff ... like a business. And I found two cheque books.' I peered at the two little books in his hand, not sure what he was talking about. 'And look,' Rory went on, 'the guy who owns the car is called Peter McCormack. His name and address are written on everything. I bet he'd give us a reward if we rang him and told him we have his stuff.'

'Yeah, and he'd ring the guards as soon as you were off the phone.'

'I'm gonna keep the stuff anyway. Like, cheques are money – maybe we could make some easy cash.'

He grabbed the empty binbag and began throwing files into it. I had a look at the kitbag that Adam had thrown aside. I took off my goalie gloves and dipped my hand in. I pulled out a pair of new football boots.

'Hey, Rory! Look.'

'Deadly!' Rory cried and then went back to bagging the files.

I put my hand in again and this time I found a pair of socks and shorts, and a brand new Man United jersey that had the name Conor written on the back of it. I held it up to show Rory. It was my size exactly.

'Hey, very nice of Adam to leave it, wasn't it?' I said. Rory came over beside me and examined the jersey a little more closely.

'Conor! Nobody called that plays for United. That must be the name of the fella who owns it. Hey, maybe you shouldn't wear it, Kev. Like, you know, just in case someone spots it on you.'

He went to tie up the black sack while I rummaged at the bottom of the kitbag. The only thing left in it was a little leather wallet with the Man United crest on it. I pulled it open but it didn't have any cash in it – only a photo. I pinched it out of its pocket and had a look at it. The photo was of a boy and a man together. The boy looked a bit like me and they were standing outside Old Trafford, cos I could see the sign. The man had his arm around the boy like a hug and they were both smiling.

'Hey, look what else I found!' Rory cried, holding up a new leather football. Then he saw the wallet.

'What's that?'

'Nothing,' I said. And when his back was turned I slid the photo back inside and then stuck the wallet in my pocket. 'Come on, Rory, let's go to my house and we'll look through everything there. Then we can decide what to keep.'

'Yeah!' Rory said, tucking the black bag under his arm. Then he stopped suddenly and peered up at the hills that rose towards the sky at the back of the estate.

'Your Adam would want to be careful all the same.'

'Why?'

'Cos someone might do a job on him up in those hills like they did to Cokey Mulligan.'

'Vigilantes, you mean.'

'Yeah. Did you not hear what they did to Cokey Mulligan?'

'I heard Ma and Sully talk about it when she was up at the Wednesday market. They were wearing balaclavas.'

'Who? Sully and your ma?'

'Yeah! Can you imagine!'

'Cokey had it coming to him!'

'That's what my ma said too, though Sully didn't agree with her. He thinks people like Cokey Mulligan should be banished out of the place.'

'Banished where?'

'I don't know. He didn't say. Maybe to some other planet on some other galaxy millions of light years away.'

Rory smiled at the thought, but then the smile faded.

'Except, Kev, he'd only wreck that place too after half an hour.'

'Yeah, but we wouldn't have to be looking at him or worrying about what he gets up to.'

'Yeah, well there's nothing much to be worried about any more. Have you seen the state of him?'

I shook my head. I didn't want to see him. I didn't want to even think about him. I turned away from the hills to have one last look at the car and I felt really sorry for Peter Whatever-his-name that owned it.

'Adam's brain must be going soft,' I said.

'Why?'

'He never torched the car.'

Rory laughed. 'I wouldn't worry about that. Don't you know it'll be well scorched by the morning.'

Then he paused and looked towards the car like he was worried about something. 'Only thing though, Kev – it's on the pitch.'

'So?'

'So if it does get torched, it's going to ruin the grass.'

'So what?'

'It's a football pitch. Like, they'll be using it at the weekend ... and look what's happened to the goalposts.'

'That's not our problem, Rory.'

'I know, but maybe I should tell my da and he might be able to get the council or the guards to come and shift it before anyone gets to it.'

'Yeah, and he'd start asking you questions about who you saw down here and who was driving the car and what would you say to that?'

'Yeah, I suppose.'

'Exactly. So you don't say anything to anyone, Rory, least of all your da.'

2

There was a brand new black Honda Civic parked outside my house. It looked like it had come straight from a garage. Rory ran towards it and peered in the driver's window like he was trying to suss out something about the owner.

'Hey, Kev! Look at these for leather seats. Who owns it do ya think? I bet it's your Aunt Rita's, hey, or maybe it's Davy's.'

'No way it's Rita's. And it's not Davy's either cos he's still got his Orion black banger. It must be someone gone in next door to see Mandy Quirke's new baby.'

Rory sprawled his arms over the body of the car and tried to give it a hug. 'I love you, car,' he said.

'Will you come on, ya looper,' I said, laughing and going in through the front door to climb the stairs to my room.

'Is that you, Kevin?' Ma called out from the kitchen.

'Yeah, me and Rory. We're just going up to my room.'

'Come in here first, will you?'

I dropped the kitbag on the floor in the hall. Rory shrugged at me and we headed towards the fag smoke drifting out the open kitchen doorway.

Ma was standing with her back to the sink, a mug of tea in one hand and a burning cigarette in the other. Uncle Davy was sitting at the table, also armed with tea and a cigarette.

'That's your car, Davy? No way!' I shouted.

'What ya think, boys eh,' Davy said, smiling and blowing two perfect smoke rings up towards the ceiling. 'A real beaut, isn't she?'

'Hey, it's deadly,' Rory said. 'Did you win the Lotto, Davy?'

'That'd be telling you now, wouldn't it,' he said, tapping the side of his nose with a finger.

'We're going down to your da's grave later and Davy's going to give us a lift,' Ma said. 'So you make sure to stay around for that, Kevin.'

'Ma, you were down there just last week.'

'Yeah, but you weren't. And neither was Adam.'

'It's your da's tenth anniversary so we have to show him he's not forgotten,' Davy said, squashing the fag end into one of Ma's cigarette saucers.

'He'd better keep his feet to himself this time,' I said.

'Who?' Ma asked.

'Da.'

'What are you talking about Kevin?' Ma said and Davy frowned at me like maybe he thought I was losing it.

'Do you not remember? Adam slipped on his arse on the wet grass and said it was Da that tripped him.'

We all laughed out loud. Adam – the eejit!

Then Ma turned her face away and her fingers found the gold chain at her neck that held Da's and her own wedding rings as well as his gold earring. She rubbed them as she peered down at the floor like as if she was remembering the day Da died in the accident at the garage. Then again, Davy looked so much like Da she must have been reminded every time he called. Maybe that's why he let his hair grow wavy and long so we all wouldn't think of Da every time we saw him. Then Ma raised her eyes again and stared at the binbag in Rory's hand.

'I hope you're not bringing more rubbish into the house,' she said.

'Oh,' Rory said, looking at the binbag like he was seeing it for the first time. His face went red as he moved it behind him to let it dangle at the back of his knees. Now we were all looking in through those knees except for stupid Rory who didn't know where to park his eyes.

'It's just stuff we found in the field,' I said.

Davy put his hand out and Rory handed him the bag. He placed the bag at his feet and opened it. He dipped his hand in and pulled out the new football. He threw it at me and I grabbed it into my stomach.

'We'll make a goalie out of you yet,' he said.

Then he began to pull out the reams of paper and the two cheque books. He looked over at Ma, who put her mug on the worktop and came nearer the table. She pushed her long straight hair behind her shoulders and leaned her head in towards the bag.

'We found them in a car –'

'We found them in the field,' I said, cutting in, annoyed now with Rory for not leaving the binbag out in the hall with the kitbag.

'A stolen car?' Ma asked.

'No!' I said as Rory the fool nodded.

'Jesus!' Ma said. 'Don't tell me that Adam –'

'Of course it wasn't Adam,' Davy said, eyeing me now like I needed a prompt to give the correct answer.

'No, Ma! It wasn't Adam. I told you we just found the stuff in the field ... it was in a car ... an old car that had been there for ages ... we saw the bag and we thought whoever owned it might like it back. That's all.'

'Yeah,' Rory said.

'And I suppose you thought they might pay you a reward if you gave it back?'

'Spot on, Davy. That's exactly what we thought,' I said.

He placed all the stuff back into the bag and then he twisted the top into a knot.

'Off ye go now. Go on!' he said and turned his back to the two of us.

Me and Rory looked at each other.

'You can't be bringing stuff from stolen cars into the house,' Ma said. 'Is that clear?'

'Yeah,' we said together, our shoulders drooping.

'Hey, Davy,' said Rory suddenly. 'Did you hear what happened to Cokey Mulligan?'

'Rory!' said Ma sharply. 'I think it's time for you to go home to your own house. Your mother must be worried about you cos you're here since early morning.'

Rory sniffed like he'd heard a joke. I threw the football at him and he caught it.

'Oh, and Davy,' he said, 'it's Kev's birthday today.'

'Jaysus! Your birthday, Kev! Of course it is.' He glanced at Ma. 'You should have reminded me, Rose.'

'I did,' Ma said as he dipped his hand in his pocket in search of cash.

'Can you believe it, he's fourteen,' Rory said and I glared at him.

Davy pulled out a few crumpled notes. He peered at them and then picked out two twenties. He smoothed them out and handed both to me.

'Here.'

I took the money, looked at it and smiled at Ma and then at Rory.

'Hey, and I'm fourteen too you know – since last week,' said Rory. I tried to give him a daggers look but he didn't read it.

'Good try, Ro,' Davy said as he put his crumpled notes back into his pocket.

'See ya, Kev!' Rory said and melted out the door.

'See ya, Uncle Davy,' I said loudly, ready to go and move the kitbag to my room before it was spotted.

Ma tapped Uncle Davy's hand where it rested on the table and he glanced up at her. She nodded towards me. Davy turned.

'Oh yeah! Great to see ya, bud!'

I looked at Ma and she gave me a little shake of her head before her eyes fell away to look for her tea. I went out into the hall, lifted the kitbag and made for the stairs. Halfway up the steps I stopped to listen.

'You shouldn't have given him so much, Davy. And what's the idea of telling them it's your car? You've only the use of it from the garage. Does your man Deegan even know you're running round in it? From what I hear he's not someone you mess with.'

'For God's sake, Rose, Trev wouldn't like you visiting him in a banger now, would he?'

'I don't think Trevor would mind if we showed up in a wheelbarrow. It's more Adam he'd have something to say about at the moment.'

'What about Adam?'

'He's selling stuff and I don't know where he's getting it from. And then there's that constant talk I hear of him involved in the joyriding that's going on. I don't want him to end up in a wheelchair like that Cokey Mulligan fella. And to cap it all he's hanging round with that Mark Madigan chap. He comes in here with Adam sometimes and never smiles or says a word to me. The lad freaks me out, Davy.'

The dishwasher door opened and I could hear the rattle

of delph and glasses as Ma sorted stuff in the top drawer. Davy coughed like he was clearing his throat.

'What if I was around more, Rose? Like, if I even moved in for a while. What do you think? Would that help?'

I leaned my head forward to hear Ma's answer but she didn't say anything. I'd liked to have seen her face so I'd have known what she was thinking.

'It makes sense, you know. It's not good to be on your own in a big estate like this. You're vulnerable. There's guys out there and they'll try and take advantage.'

Now it was Ma's turn to clear her throat.

'Thanks, Davy. I appreciate the offer, I do, but – I think I'm doing OK. I still have a little bit of money left from the accident. Kevin's a pet and Adam can be difficult, I know, but he's got a soft heart. He acts tough but he's not really. He's just a bit lost.'

'Then all the more reason to have me here,' Davy said.

Ma didn't say anything immediately.

'I don't think they'd want anyone else moving in,' she said at last.

'It's ten years, Rose. Ten years without a man in your life. And look at you. You're still young and ... still a looker.'

Ma laughed out loud. 'Alright, Davy! You're not selling cars now, you know, so you can leave off the palaver.'

The delph and glasses gave a rattle as Ma rolled the top shelf back inside the dishwasher and banged the door shut. 'Anyway you should be out there impressing some other woman, especially now you've a flash car to parade around in.'

'I'm not interested in any other woman. And anyway not every woman wants to be involved with a jailbird, you know.'

'That's all history, Davy. Very few people round here know anything about it. And if I was you I wouldn't be mentioning it to a prospective partner.'

There was silence, then the hiss and flush of water as the dishwasher rumbled to life.

'I like spending time here, Rose – with the lads, with you.'

There was silence for a few seconds like Ma needed time to compose her answer.

'I like you spending time with them, Davy. I do. If you don't mind you could spend a little more time here then, during the day, with Adam ... see if you can soften him a bit.'

'I can do that, Rose. But you don't want him soft. Not around here.'

I heard the back door opening and I thought it might be Adam coming in. But it wasn't.

'Where are you going with that?' Davy asked.

'I'm not leaving a bag of rubbish in my kitchen. I'm putting it in the bin so it doesn't bring more trouble down on top of me.'

'Leave it!'

'Leave it?'

'That's what I said. I'll take it.'

'Where?'

'I'll bring it back to whoever owns it. The name and address is in there.'

'You're joking me?'

'I'm serious. I'll bring it back and drop it at their door.'

'Are you going to sell it back to them?'

'Ah now, Rose. That's a bit mean. I'll bring it back. I'm sure whoever owns it will be grateful.'

Ma mustn't have heard the hurt in his voice cos she laughed like she didn't really believe that he'd any intention of returning the stuff.

'Look!' Davy said. 'See these hands. See them? Remember how greasy they'd be when me and Trev worked in the garage. Look at them now, spotless after years slaving in her majesty's prison laundry. I've washed myself clean, Rose. I have. I really have, even though you don't like the calibre of people I do business with.'

I could picture Uncle Davy standing there in the kitchen with his palms held up in front of his chest, standing like he was some holy statue, like one of the saints that Ma had turned Da into.

But I got a shock when I heard about Davy in prison. Any time I had asked Ma about him, she always said he was sorting himself out in Manchester and he'd come home when he was ready. I was so excited when he did come back and he was so much fun to have around. I remembered how one time in school I'd gotten an essay to write about people I admired and I'd written a bit about Davy. And when I was writing it I noticed that the first two letters of his name spelled 'Da'. And I did wonder what it might be like having him full-time in the house. But Ma's answer was definite, like she knew something I didn't know. And

22

I wasn't sure I wanted it to happen now either. The mention of prison kinda rattled me and I wouldn't be able to ask about it either cos Ma would know I was earwigging.

Davy started to talk to Ma about Da's grave and about flowers and doing it up so I stood up and made my way quietly to my room, feeling worried but not sure about what.

3

Davy took the day off work and turned up the following morning at ten o'clock as if to show Ma he was serious about spending time in the house. I made him his mug of tea the way he liked it, the way he said Da liked it: strong with two sugars and no milk.

When Adam eventually surfaced, Davy took him off out to put new white stones on Da's grave, with Adam complaining that he didn't still have the new Honda to drive him around in. And when they came back, Adam took him up to his room and spent the next couple of hours showing Davy his latest computer game and giving him lessons on how to play it. But Davy was always keen to look for Ma to join him when he took his smoke or his tea break. And Ma did join him for a couple of them and she laughed at his jokes but I didn't hear her slag him now like she did before.

The following day Adam was already up when Davy called and took him off to a breakers yard to try and find

new hub-caps for his car. Ma laughed when I said Davy
was a great man for the graveyards.

When they came back and Davy came into the kitchen
looking for Ma's company I made him a cup of tea again
and took the letters off his name in my head and pretended
he was Da. And when he saw me watching him he winked
at me and said, 'All right, bud?' and I said, 'Yeah,' and let
him be Davy again.

Later on that day himself and Adam sat out in the
garden, both wearing shades and looking like each other
with their slicked-back black hair, their white T-shirts and
their khaki shorts. They were drinking cans and smoking
and Ma called me over to have a look. I could only smirk
at the state of them.

'Ma, their skinny white legs are like candles,' I said.

Ma laughed out loud.

'Does Da even know what suntan lotion is?'

Ma laughed even louder.

'You called him Da!'

'I did not, Ma!'

'You did!'

'I didn't. I know I didn't.'

I was going to move away when she touched my shoulder.

'Are you OK with this?'

'What?'

'Your uncle ... about the house more.'

'Well, it doesn't mean you're going to marry him or
anything, does it?'

'What? Would you like something like that to happen?'

'Ma! Will you stop!'

'It's just nice for Adam,' Ma said, smiling out into the garden and waving at Davy who had spotted us watching. 'Hey, and it'll be nice for us too, Kevin, if he's able to keep Adam out of trouble. And I notice that Madser chap seems to stay away when Davy is here.'

'Maybe that's because he knows something about Davy the rest of us don't know.' I didn't look at Ma but I could feel her eyes watching me. Then she sighed and shook her head as if perhaps she was expecting too much from Davy's presence.

On the following day I got up late and hadn't heard Davy arrive. I walked in on him and Adam when they were in the sitting room. Uncle Davy was on his knees with the bag from the field in front of him. He had spilled all the mess of paper on the floor and was sorting through it. Adam was asleep on the couch with his feet up and his head on his chest, drooling into his phone. Davy didn't even notice me come in, he was that busy sorting the stuff, so I stood right beside him and he glanced up at me.

'Howya, bud,' he said and went back to his work.

'Hey, Davy, do you know how to play chess?'

Davy moved bits of paper around on the floor like he was sorting jigsaw pieces.

'I know the rules Kevin, and I played a bit … when I was in Manchester. But I'm a bit rusty now though.'

'I could teach you some moves,' I said.

I heard a snigger from the couch and when I glanced over I could see Adam wide awake now and thumb-tapping his phone.

'It's all right, Kevin,' Davy said. 'I don't really have the patience for it. It used to do my head in when I was playing some dozy snail-brain who needed half a day to make a move.'

'Short Arse.' Adam coughed into his hand and then smirked down at his game.

'Davy! Will you say something to him? He's still calling me names.'

Davy frowned over at Adam.

'What? What did I do now?' Adam huffed.

'You're calling me names and Ma told you to stop.'

'What are you saying to him?' Davy said, sounding cross.

'I'm not saying anything.'

'He keeps calling me Short Arse.'

'Short Arse? Is that what you're saying?'

'I called him Short Arms, that's all. He needs to get his hearing checked out.'

'Short Arms! That's not too bad, Kev. Jesus, you should hear what I was called when I was ... when I was your age. Or the names we invented for the teachers we had.'

'Hey! That's right!' Adam said, sitting up. 'Didn't Da used call you Dipper cos you were always getting into trouble for robbing stuff.'

Uncle Davy turned and gave Adam a look I'd never seen on his face before. It was like his eyes narrowed and turned cold. Adam froze, then nervously glanced at me like I should back him up but I was enjoying the moment too much to offer anything.

'Don't know where you heard that crap, Adam, but I'm telling you one thing. Nobody ever called me a name I didn't like a second time.' Then he lowered his head and went back to concentrating on the papers. I looked over at Adam and grinned in triumph.

'Short Arse!' he mouthed quietly back at me.

'Davy! He's saying it again.'

'What?' Adam cried and jumped up to his feet. 'Now I can't even talk into my phone?'

'Cut it out, Adam,' Davy said, and Adam sighed and sat back down again. Davy turned his eyes on me and I could see that some of the coldness was still there in them.

'But you need to harden up, Kevin. If someone calls you names you come back at them with a better one.'

'What? So I can call him names then?'

'That's the way it works.'

'But if I call him names like, for instance, MISTER SPOCK – he's going to lose the cool and try to kill me.'

Adam shot up on the couch and looked ready to attack me.

Davy laughed.

'See what I mean, Kev. Direct hit.' Then he pointed his finger at Adam. 'And you! You've your da's ears so get over it.'

'He calls me that again and he's dead.'

'All right, just give it a rest, both of you,' Davy said, holding up a piece of paper that looked just like one of Ma's bank statements.

Adam got back to his game and I stood watching Davy.

'Are you really bringing it back?'

'Yeah,' he said, not looking up.

'Do you want me to help you?'

'He's very good at sorting,' Adam said. 'He spent two years in Junior Infants and now he's able to help Ma sort out socks.'

'Davy!'

'It's all right, Kevin. I nearly have it done so go and help your ma in the kitchen.'

I glared over at Adam who was sniggering into his phone and then I watched Davy some more in case he changed his mind about needing help.

'Some people have money to burn and an easy life,' he mumbled, like he was talking to himself. 'And some of us have nothing at all just because of one lousy mistake.'

I didn't like to hear Davy talk like that or see that look in his eyes, so I left him to his sorting. I hung outside the door to hear what else might get said.

'Ma has him ruined,' Adam said. 'He's like her pet kitten or something.'

Davy didn't say anything and I hoped it was because he was too busy concentrating on his sorting and not because he agreed with him.

But it was like after that day Uncle Davy seemed to grow suddenly tired of sitting around the house. The next day when he called it was much later and he didn't talk as much, and once or twice I heard him snap at Adam, telling him to stop with all his jabber. I think Davy was hoping that if he helped with Adam then Ma might reward him by giving him a bit of extra attention. But if he was he must have been disappointed, cos I never heard Ma suggest even once that she and him would do anything together on their own.

Sometimes when I watched Davy, I'd try really hard to remember him and Da from when I was small. I can't remember much about either of them though because Da died when I was four and Davy went off to England shortly afterwards. But I have this one memory that I once thought was about Da but I know now is really about Davy.

I'm four or five and should be in school but I'm not. And now I think it's because it was shortly after Da died and Ma was keeping me at home. I'm in the kitchen and she's watching me colour in a picture of an elephant with lots of different crayons.

But then there's a ring on the doorbell and when Ma comes back there's a woman with her from the school and she starts talking to me and saying lovely things about the elephant and staying inside the lines and I think she means lions. Then she sits down and speaks to Ma about me going back to school and I know she's making her feel sad and I want to let a big roar at her.

Then the doorbell rings again and I go over towards the kitchen door to look out and suddenly a man comes bursting out of the sitting room and goes racing up the stairs. He's wearing a hoodie with the hood up so I'm not sure who he is but I think it's Da. Then the front door bangs open and four big guards come charging in and go stamping up the stairs and when I look behind me I can see Ma and the woman from the school with big shocked faces on them, cos they didn't know Da was hiding in there either.

We listen and hear shouting from upstairs and the four guards come charging thump-thump-thump-thump back down again. The last guard says Da flew out the window and then he slips on the steps and falls on his arse and then bounces up quickly like the stairs is made of rubber and he follows the other three out the front door. And then they're gone and the door is closed and I go back to colouring in the elephant, knowing now how Da had disappeared off up into heaven.

I was thinking about all that, waiting for Rory to call for me to go to the Friday night chess club. Ma sent him up to my room when he arrived. He had a Man U mug that he gave me for my birthday and he had the football with him.

I had the wallet with the photo of the boy and his father in my back pocket, and I had changed into my new black tracksuit bottoms and grey zipped hoodie top that Ma had bought me for my birthday. The only other birthday present I got was a maths set that Becky Norton called over with. She pretended it wasn't a present at all, like she didn't even know it was my birthday. She said her ma had picked up two for the price of one down in Eason's and I could have the second one, especially cos I was good at maths, and we'd both still be in the same maths group.

Rory sat at my table and was examining the contents of the box.

'Hey, you've got some of your gear already,' he said, lifting out the metal compass and prodding his finger with the spike, like to see how sharp it was.

'Yeah, Ma just bought it today – two for the price of one.'

'Deadly! Hey, can I have the other one?'

'The other what?'

'The other set. Like, you're not going to need two, are you?'

I could feel my face go red. There was no way I was going to tell him about getting it as a present from Becky Norton cos I'd never hear the end of the slagging.

'I don't know what she did with it, Rory. I think she gave it to someone.'

'Who?'

'I don't know, Rory. But what do you want it for anyway unless you're thinking of giving it to someone?'

'Who would I give it to?'

'Hey, don't think I haven't noticed, Rory. You probably want to give it to Mags Boylan cos I know you fancy her.'

'Hey, that reminds me,' Rory said getting to his feet and pulling his phone from the pocket of his jeans. 'Wait till you see what she sent me?' He flicked through photos and then pointed the screen at me. 'She sent me that selfie yesterday. Jesus, look at her the way she's changed. She's like a model. And she's just wearing her new school jumper and, hey, I don't know if she's got anything underneath it. And do you know what she wrote?'

'What?'

He turned the screen around and read it out loud.

'Shoulda got the next size up. What u think?' Rory pushed the phone against his heart and closed his eyes and sighed loudly.

'Mags Boylan sent you that?'

'Yeah. And she wants one back from me.'

'Mags Boylan is a big mouth, Rory, and she's full of herself.'

'Yeah but look at that face – and that jumper.'

I glanced at the too tight jumper, annoyed cos it only made me think of me having to wear the old manky leprechaun green one that still fit me from last year.

Rory sighed once more at the photo then put the phone back in his pocket and lifted up the maths set.

'Becky Norton,' he said suddenly.

'What about her?'

'Becky Norton. I bet that's who you're keeping the other set for. Ya sly yoke ya, Kev.'

'Will you shut up, Rory. I don't fancy Becky Norton and she doesn't fancy me.'

I went and sat on my bed to let him know I didn't want to talk any more about school, or Becky Norton. What I wanted to talk about instead was the car and all the stuff we'd found. The kitbag was under the bed. I had tried on all the gear, including the boots, and everything fitted me like they were really bought for me.

Rory rolled the football onto the bed.

'What did you bring that for? We're going to play chess and anyway I thought you were going to keep it in your house.'

'I don't want it.'

'Why not? It's practically new.'

'I just don't want it, OK.'

'Well I already have a ball, Rory.'

'I know.'

'Yeah, well then I don't need a second one and I've got all the other stuff.'

'That's just it.'

'What? You're pissed off cos I got more stuff than you?'

'No. I don't want any of your stuff.'

'Then what's wrong?'

'I think we should give everything back.'

'What!'

'We should give all the gear back – the football, the boots, the rest of the gear, everything.'

'Are you crazy?' I said.

'It's not right, Kev. It just doesn't feel right.'

'What are you talking about? You love free stuff. You're always taking stuff.'

'I know. But this time, I don't want the ball. I just don't want it. There's something wrong about it.'

'Wrong?'

'Yeah. Like whoever owned that car, they must train a team. And my da – remember? He used to train us when we were under seven.'

'This is different.'

'How is it different?'

'Because ... because if we didn't take all that stuff then it would've just got burned with everything else. And the car did get burned. Did you see what was left of it?'

'I don't care,' Rory said. 'You should still give it back.'

I thought of the boots and how they fitted and how deadly I looked in all the gear when I stood in front of the mirror.

'And the jersey. It obviously belongs to someone called Conor. It's his jersey – what happens if he sees you wearing it?'

'All right! Just shut up, OK?'

'So you're going to give it back?'

'How do I know where he lives?'

'I know,' Rory said. 'The name of the club was written on the bibs. Glen Rovers. I know where they play. My da brought me out there once to watch a match. It's out near the Glen River Estate on the 75 bus.'

'Well, thanks very much, Rory. Just thanks very much. OK?'

'What?'

'You and your stupid da, and watching stupid matches. I'll think about it tomorrow. OK? First we have to go and play chess and this time I'm going to beat the crap out of ya.'

4

I never thought I'd like chess. I thought chess was for geeks. But Sully made it fun to play and then it was brilliant when me and Rory were the best at it, cos we're pretty crap at most other games. And Sully bought these big plastic chess boards that roll up, and plastic chessmen that are smooth and lovely to handle cos they're just the right size for your fingers to hold. And I love the names of the pieces and how they all move differently and place themselves like an army, with the poor doomed pawns in the front line, like those soldiers in the trenches we learned about in school. And we had a laugh too when Rory kept calling the pawns 'prawns' and Sully giving out to us when we kept calling the knight a horse.

'Hey, Rory,' I said on our way to the club, 'if you were a chess piece, what piece would you be?'

'The king! Definitely the king – you know, cos the king is the most powerful.'

'Yeah but he's a lazy prick though, isn't he?'

Rory laughed. 'And, Kev, I think you'd have to be the knight with your big horse's head on you.'

'The knight's what I'd like to be, smartarse! But I don't think you could make king, Rory. I think with your pointy head, you'd have to be a bishop.'

Rory opened his mouth to say something but then the two of us just stopped and stared towards the community centre. We knew straight away that something bad had happened. A squad car was parked up on the path, with the blue light swirling, and all the teenagers who should have been inside the centre were gathered in a huddle outside trying to see in through the glass doors.

Becky was there. She gave me a little worried smile and a tiny wave when she saw me running towards her. I gave her a little wave back that nobody saw.

'What's going on?' I asked her.

Heads turned to look at me, then turned away – all except for Mags Boylan, who stared straight at me like it was all my fault or something.

'Someone broke in and wrecked the place,' Becky said, 'so we all have to go home.'

'Someone!' Mags Boylan said, like I was supposed to know what she meant.

I shoved my way into the middle of the huddle and pushed open the door.

'You're not allowed in there!' Mags Boylan shouted after me.

When I got inside the second set of doors, I stopped dead at the state of the two new leather sofas that Sully had bought for the lobby area. All the stuffing was sticking out like guts in a zombie film, like someone had slashed the black leather with a knife.

I hurried past them and into the café area. The floor near one wall was covered in what looked like shells, but when I got closer and poked at the mess with my foot I could make out the shape of broken cups, plates and saucers. The wall opposite was covered in graffiti that said 'Sully is a peedo', and a drawing of a giant willy beside it. Tables and chairs were knocked over, and Coke and orange juice had been spilled and cartons of milk stamped on and exploded.

There was a plastic chess board folded in half on the floor under one of the tables. I went over to pick it up. But it wasn't folded over at all. It was a piece from a board that had been sliced in half.

'Aw no – NO!' I cried, staring ahead towards the games room and afraid to go any further cos I knew what I'd see in there. But I headed for the door anyway, holding my arms high to not touch anything.

When I leaned my head into the room I could see Sully was in there, rubbing his forehead and talking to a guard who was writing in a little notebook. Brendan and Sarah who worked in the club were down at the end of the room. They had mops in their hands and a bucket on the floor between them. They all looked up when they heard me come in. I held up the piece of plastic for them to see.

'Not now, Kevin,' Sully said, waving me away. The guard gave me a big frowny face and I could see it wasn't a good time to ask any questions. I went back out to the other room and Rory and Mags Boylan were there and she had her hand clamped onto Rory's arm like she owned him. Then she broke away from Rory and went to pick up one of the chairs.

'Don't touch anything,' I shouted at her. 'They'll want to get fingerprints.'

'Yeah, well you know whose prints they'll find?'

'Who?'

'Your Adam's!'

I glanced towards Rory. He shrugged. I glared at Mags, daring her to say it again.

'What are you going on about?'

'It was Adam who did this! They're all saying it outside. He was here today and got thrown out cos he was trying to steal Coke.'

'That's a lie!' I shouted. She looked towards Rory like she was expecting him to back her up.

'She's not lying, Kevin,' Rory said. 'It was Adam. You know it was.'

I don't know why I did what I did next but I just lost the cool, the way Rory took her side and made me feel like a stranger. I threw the piece of plastic at his face and then I jumped at him and he slipped on the wet floor and fell back on a chair and I fell and landed on top of him. I grabbed his hair and pulled it and I didn't care if it all came out of his stupid pointy head. And I didn't care either that Mags Boylan was girly screaming for me to get off him.

Then I felt a hand grabbing me by the collar of my jacket and haul me upwards, making me choke. When I looked round I could see it was Sully who was holding me and he looked really pissed off but he let go of me quickly when he saw that he'd hurt me.

'What the hell are you doing, Kevin? Don't you think I've enough on my plate without the two of you fighting?'

Rory was trying not to cry and holding his head but I didn't care.

'They're blaming Adam for all this.'

Sully looked at Rory who was sniffing now and trying to stuff the tears back into his eyes with his knuckles.

'He did do it,' Mags Boylan whined. 'Everyone knows he did!'

'See? They're still saying it.'

The guard was about to say something but Sully put up his hand to let him know he was dealing with it.

'Look, Kevin. Adam was here earlier and there was trouble over a can of Coke, and he ... well ... he said he'd be back. And someone said the graffiti in the games room is like his writing. That's all. But the guards will sort it out.'

'The guards couldn't sort out socks!' I shouted, and then I picked up the sliced piece of plastic chess board and barged past Rory and Mags Boylan and headed for the outside door.

Becky was waiting outside. Everyone else was gone home. I didn't know if she was waiting for me or for Rory and Mags. I don't know why she'd bother waiting for Mags though, cos of the way she and her mates call her Specky Becky and think it's hilarious.

'My brother was in there too, wasn't he?'

'Yeah, more than likely,' I said. 'But it's Adam gets blamed for everything like it's just him on his own.'

I didn't wait to hear what she'd say to that. I didn't care what she'd say, even if she had been waiting just for me. I walked off and headed for home.

5

Uncle Davy's old Orion banger was outside the house.

'Davy!' I shouted as soon as I opened the door.

'In here!' Ma's voice came from the kitchen.

But Davy wasn't in there with her.

'Where's Uncle Davy?

Ma put down the magazine she was reading.

'What's wrong?' she said.

'Adam broke into the community centre with his mates and they wrecked the place, and all the chess boards are sliced. Look!'

I threw the useless piece of plastic on the table.

'How do they know it was Adam?'

'It was Adam! His stupid writing's on the wall.'

'What writing? What wall?'

'Ma! There's graffiti on one of the walls in the centre and everyone is saying it's Adam's handwriting.'

'And that's all they have – writing?'

'Ma, it was him. I know it was. He got thrown out earlier cos he tried to steal a can of Coke.'

'When did this break-in happen?'

'I don't know. When the centre was closed. Some time this evening.'

Ma went over to the sink and looked out into the back garden like she was trying to think. Then she turned around and stared at me.

'Listen to me! As far as you and I are concerned, Adam was here all evening. OK? And if you didn't see him, well, I did.'

'But Ma, that's not true!'

'And is it true what they're saying about him? How do they know for sure? They don't. But they'll pick on Adam because, what – he tried to take a can of Coke?'

'Where's Uncle Davy?' I asked.

'He was here earlier but I don't know where he is now.'

'His car is outside.'

'Listen, Kevin. Your uncle doesn't need to hear about this. OK?'

I couldn't believe Ma was letting Adam get away with it. She was always letting him away with stuff. It wasn't fair.

'Ma, do you know he's got boxes and boxes of cigarettes up in his room? He's selling them round the houses for Uncle Davy. Yeah, Ma! Uncle Davy! And the Quirkes buy off him and they shouldn't even be smoking. And he goes into town selling. Did you know that?'

Ma's eyes glanced towards her cigarette packet on the table and then she turned away to look out into the garden again.

'I can't believe you're not going to say anything, Ma. I just can't believe it!'

I tore out the door and raced down the path towards the cul-de-sac at the back of our road. That's where I knew Adam would be. He'd be where they always hung out – in the deserted house at the end of the cul-de-sac. African people had lived there but then moved off somewhere else and the council boarded it up until they fixed it for the next family. But no family seemed to want to live in it, so Adam and his mates broke in the back door, took down the boards blocking the kitchen window and were now using the place as a den.

I went round the back of the house and saw Lunchbox. He was standing on the step, leaning on a crutch and peeing into the long grass. He half-turned when he heard me coming and peed down the front of his tracksuit bottoms.

'For feck's sake!' he shouted as I went past him and in through the open door.

Adam and Madser were in the kitchen. Adam was sitting in a wheelchair that he must have stolen from somewhere and Madser was on an old armchair that Ma had thrown out. Both of them had their backs to me. In the middle of the room was a white plastic garden table with five or six tall towers on it made out of Coke cans. Adam and Madser were smoking and playing cards. Adam had his hoodie on, so I grabbed it and I yanked him backwards.

He toppled over and, as he fell, he kicked out at the table and the towers of Coke came crashing down.

'What the hell!' Madser yelled. I jumped on Adam and I started to belt him with my fists. I could hear Madser and Lunchbox screeching their mad laughs as Adam tried to grab me by the arms and pull me off.

'Get off me, ya little thick!' he roared, and Lunchbox's and Madser's squeals of laughter got even louder. But it wasn't funny at all.

Adam pushed me away and into the table. When we got to our feet, the two of us just stopped still and stared at the doorway. Davy was standing there.

'What the hell is he doing here?' Davy said, looking at me.

'The little looper tried to kill me.'

Lunchbox and Madser were staring now like statues with their mouths open, but Davy eyed them and nodded towards the garden and the two of them vanished out the door.

'I'll kill him!' Adam said, making a fist and moving towards me. But Davy put up his free hand and it stopped Adam in his tracks.

'What are you doing here, Kevin?'

'Adam broke into the community centre and destroyed all our games.'

'It wasn't me, Davy. I wasn't anywhere near that shitty place.'

'You wrote on the wall, you stupid thick – and where did all those cans of Coke come from then?'

Davy grabbed me by the arm and swung me around so I was looking up at him.

'Will ya just shut up, Kevin, and let me sort this out?'

'But Da– '

'Just ... shut it, Kevin.'

Adam was about to shout something at me but Davy pointed his finger at him like it was the barrel of a gun. Adam went quiet, even though I could see he was ready to explode.

'I'll sort Adam out. You go home.'

'He's going to lie.'

'What did I just say? I'll sort it out.'

I turned and gave Adam a big cheesy smile before I headed for the door and I could see he was afraid to say anything cos he knew Davy would lose it with him.

'Thanks, Uncle Davy,' I said real loud and then I left them there.

Lunchbox and Madser were outside the door ear-wigging but I just walked past them like they weren't even there.

'Hey, Tiger!' Madser called after me but I just kept on walking. I could still hear their loud mad laughter from out on the road.

When I got back home Ma called me into the kitchen. 'Mr Sullivan was here,' she said.

'What did he want?'

'Look!' She was pointing to a plastic shopping bag on the table. I opened the bag and looked in.

'He brought them here especially for you, Kevin. He said he'd rescued one set and knew you'd like to have it. And he said he was sorry if he was cross with you earlier. And I told him it wasn't Adam that broke in. Adam wouldn't do that to stuff that's important to you.'

I wasn't really listening to Ma now at all. I took out the plastic chess board and then spilled all the chess pieces onto the table. Ma watched me as I placed the pieces in their positions – the lines of little pawns facing each other at the front with the heavy hitters in the back row ready to protect their king.

'Show me how to play,' Ma said.

I looked at her and snorted. 'Ma, come off it. You'd never have the patience.'

'Just show me, OK?'

So I showed her. And as I showed her I realised why it is I like chess so much. It calms me. It calms me so I can forget everything except the game. That's why I forgot all about Adam as I told Ma about the pawns and how they could move either one or two places forward on their first move. But after that they could take only one cautious step at a time because now they were really heading into danger. I showed her how the little fat rooks can scoot up and down the lines at the side like wingers in football. I thought of Rory as I showed her the bishop with his pointy head and I told her he kinda lurks and then sweeps out to grab you like a spider on his diagonal web if you wander into his radar. I showed her the powerful queen but warned her that if you lose her early in the game, then it's like you're in a fight with your best soldier gone.

I explained how a stalemate happened and how if you couldn't get out of check, then it was checkmate and the game was over. And she was amazed when I told her you could move your king out of trouble by getting him to swap places with the rook. You could only make this move once in a game, though. I told Ma it was called 'castling'. And Ma laughed out loud when I called the king a lazy bastard cos he just sits there being minded all the time, or when he does bother to move his arse, he'll just take one step in any direction to keep himself out of danger.

'He makes everyone else travel all over the shop to protect him, and at the same time they have to hunt down the other king – and the bravest of the pawns with a bit of luck can one day become queen but nobody, no matter what they do, can ever become king.'

'You'd make a great teacher,' Ma said, but she probably changed her mind when she saw how I nearly lost the cool trying to explain to her how the knight made his little L-shaped jumps backwards and forwards. But she got the hang of it eventually and we were chilled out in the middle of a game when Uncle Davy and Adam walked in the door.

'Hey, guys, look. Kevin is showing me how to play chess.'

Adam barely looked at the board. He stood in the doorway pretending to read something on his phone. Davy went to the kettle and poured water into it.

'Can we get chips, Ma?' Adam asked.

'Chips?'

'Yeah, Ma. I'm starving.'

'For Christ's sake,' Davy snapped, staring at Ma. 'Do you do any cooking in this house at all?'

Ma opened her mouth like she was going to snap something back at him, but then she closed it again.

'You could have chips too, Uncle Davy,' I said.

Davy stared at me like he'd just spotted me in the room. Then he noticed the chess pieces.

'Where did all that come from?'

'Sully brought it round,' I said, looking at Adam to see if he was still ignoring it.

Davy dropped the kettle and it clattered into the sink. Then he went and got the bin and swiped the chess board and all the pieces into it like they were the worst kind of rubbish. He banged the bin back down into the corner beside the cooker and turned his angry eyes on us.

'Are ye stupid or what? The centre gets robbed and Adam gets blamed for it. So what's going to happen when the cops come round and see that chess crap? What are they going to say? They're going to wonder how it got here, aren't they? Adam must have stolen it, they'll say. That's right, they'll stitch him up like they like to stitch everyone up.'

'But Uncle Davy ... that's –'

'Just shut it, OK? I've had enough from you for one day.' Then he glared at Ma. 'Make some tea for feck's sake! Or do you not even want to do that much for me?'

He barged past Ma and went into the sitting room. Ma just stood at the table with her head bowed and a hand over her mouth like she might get sick. Then she turned to stare at Adam like he might have something to say for himself. But it was like he was struck dumb and could only gaze at the sitting room door that Uncle Davy had banged shut behind him.

I left the kitchen and went up to my room. Quirke's new baby was bawling next door, so I turned on the telly but hardly even noticed what was on.

Then I heard movement at the door and I got a fright, but it was only Ma, standing there, peering in at me.

'Where is he?' I asked.

'He's gone back out.'

'Good.'

I didn't say anything else, just turned the TV up louder. Ma looked to see what I was watching. A lab guy was cutting up a woman's body and talking to a detective about what he had found in her stomach. 'Are you sure it's a good idea to be watching that stuff at this hour? It'll give you nightmares.'

'It's only *CSI*. You used to let Adam watch worse and he was only twelve.'

'And look where that got me.'

If Ma expected me to laugh, then I wasn't going to please her. She moved towards the bed. I pulled the cover over my head.

'All right, Kevin. I'm going,' she said.

I could hear her move towards the door. I pulled the cover down and stared at her back.

'How come you never told me he did time?'

'What are you talking about, Kevin?'

'Ma, I know, so don't pretend. I heard it on the street.'

'That was years ago, Kevin, and I don't want to talk about it. Anyway it doesn't have anything to do with what happened down in the kitchen. Your Uncle Davy has a bit of a temper, that's all. He gets frustrated because life didn't turn out for him the way it did for your da.'

'He's alive, isn't he? And he has us. And he shouldn't be talking to you like that. He shouldn't be talking like that in this house. And if he's like that with me and you then he's not going to be much good with Adam. He's only going to make him worse.'

I let my head fall back onto the pillow and I stared up at the stain on the ceiling. It looked like a head with two faces on it.

'He gets like this from time to time. Maybe it's to do with the time he spent in prison, I dunno. But he's making every effort to put it behind him. And for your da's sake I have to give him a chance. Come on, Kev, give him a break. He's got no one else besides us.'

'Yeah,' I said, and I started watching the lab guy make

another cut on the dead body like he was just cutting paper. Ma sighed and stared at me and then at the telly.

'Don't have that too loud.'

'I know, Ma,' I said. 'The baby.'

She sighed again and then she headed out of the room, closing the door quietly behind her. I listened but I didn't hear her go back downstairs. I turned the telly up, even though I didn't want to watch the stupid thing at all. Rory said he has to read a book in bed cos his ma won't let him have his laptop or his phone in his room. Rory's ma is a sap sometimes.

6

Rory's baldy-headed da drove a taxi. (Rory said the reason he shaved all his hair off was because he was going bald. Me and Rory thought that was hilarious.) The taxi was a big fat grey six-seater Hyundai van. It was parked in the drive of his house with the gate locked up tight against the back of it to keep it safe. Rory's cat, Moppy, sat sunning herself on a plastic chair by the front step.

I hopped the wall, gave Moppy's head a gentle rub and then rang the bell, hoping it would be Rory's ma or Rory who would answer. But it was his baldy-headed da who opened the door, and from the eye he gave me, I knew I wasn't welcome.

'What do you want, Kevin?'

'I just want to talk to Rory.'

'I hope you came to apologise.'

'Yeah,' I said. I hadn't thought of doing that, but what else could I say? Rory's da was a huge man. He would have made a deadly wrestler if he hadn't got so soft from sitting so long in his taxi.

He called out Rory's name and then he disappeared into the house. He didn't invite me in or crack any jokes like he usually did. I turned round towards the green and watched the small kids playing football and using the mini football posts that Rory's da had made for them.

'What do you want, Kevin?'

When I saw Rory's face I got a shock. He had a black eye.

'Hey! I didn't do that?'

'You did.'

'I thought I just pulled your hair.'

'You got me with your elbow,' Rory said, holding the door with one hand, like any second he was going to close it.

'I'm sorry, Rory. I'm sorry. I just called to tell you that … to tell you I'm bringing all the football gear back to that place where you said.'

'OK,' Rory said, but he didn't let go of the door.

'Can I come in?'

'My da said you're not allowed – and I'm not allowed out.'

'I'm bringing the stuff back, Rory. And I thought you might come with me. Just to show me where it is.'

'You know where it is, Kevin.'

His da's voice called him and he glanced over his shoulder.

'I have to go,' he said, and closed the door.

'I'm not like Adam,' I shouted. 'I'm not! I'm bringing it all back and I'll come back for you when I've done it.'

Something brushed against my leg and when I looked down I saw it was Moppy looking for me to lift her.

'I'm not like him, Moppy. I'm not. You know I'm not like him.'

7

I took the 75 bus and sat upstairs with the kitbag but no real plan. I didn't bring the football. I didn't think Conor, whoever he was, would miss the football as much as the other stuff.

I got off the bus near the Glen River Shopping Centre like Rory said I should. I could see where a carnival had taken over a grassy area at the back of the car park. There was a poster on the bus shelter advertising it with 'Freak Out' written on it, and a picture of the ride underneath. But I walked fast past it and towards the pitches. A game had already started on one of them but it looked like a kids' match. I followed the railings until I came to a gate that led in to a small car park and a sign that said 'GLEN RIVER ROVERS'.

There was nobody around, except for a woman in a black tracksuit who was lifting a heavy-looking canvas bag out of the boot of a silver Beemer. I walked past her, pretending to read a message on my phone, and headed for the first of the changing rooms.

The changing room was empty – just bare walls with hooks and wooden benches. Then I heard a noise behind me.

'Hey! Well done. You're early.'

I turned around and saw it was the woman from the car park. She had a big smiley round face and now had her blonde hair tied back with a scrunchie the way Ma sometimes ties hers when she's busy and it's getting in her way.

'What?'

'You're the goalie?'

'I am, sometimes.'

'Yvonne sent you, then. Well, fair play to her. I wasn't sure she'd remember.' She must have seen the puzzled look on my face. 'You are a goalie, aren't you? Please tell me you're a goalie.'

'Yeah!'

'Wonderful. Now I won't have to get into a fight with Conor.'

'Conor?'

'He's my son. He'll be here in a minute.'

She stared at the bag at my feet.

'And you brought your gear.'

Her eyes didn't move from the bag. I felt my face go red to match it.

'Another Red Devil. Conor will be pleased about that as well.' She turned away to find where she'd left her team kitbag. She picked it up and spilled all the gear out into a neat pile on the floor. 'Good news is you won't need any of your own, just your boots, because I've a lovely yellow goalie jersey here for you, and the rest of the kit as well – gloves, even.'

I stared at her, not sure exactly what I was after landing myself in.

'Hey, forgive me. I do rattle on so. My name is Jenny and I'm ... I'm ... well, it doesn't matter, just call me Jenny.'

Then I could hear crunching on the stones outside and five or six boys all arrived into the changing room and Jenny made a big fuss of greeting each of them. She said their names as she shook their hands, but I could see from the way they lowered their eyes that they were feeling embarrassed.

'Is Conor not coming?' I heard one of them ask.

'He's just gone to the toilet. He'll be here in a minute. But look who I have here! It's ...'

'Kevin,' I said.

'Kevin, our new goalie.'

I could see from the way they looked me up and down they were thinking I was too small. Then they lost interest and sat and laughed and chatted and slagged each other and I kept an eye on the door.

'Conor!' Jenny said as soon as she saw him.

It was the boy from the photo I'd found in the wallet. There was no doubt about it. As soon as I saw him, I lowered the yellow jersey and let it rest on the kitbag, covering it. He looked exactly the same except his hair was a little bit shorter, and with the same spiky style as my own. He was about the same size as me, so I knew why he mightn't want to stand in goal.

'Say hi to Kevin,' Jenny called out to him. 'Now you don't have to worry about being the keeper. Isn't that great?'

Conor glanced over at me and nodded, then went to the spilled pile of jerseys on the floor and selected the number 10.

More boys came in and Jenny had to raise her voice to get everyone to quieten down while she pulled out a sheet of paper from her tracksuit top and read out the team. The paper shook in her hand and you could tell she was really nervous.

Conor had moved to a corner of the changing room that was well away from me, but I kept a close eye on him as I sneaked out the boots and put them on. And when I had them on, I waited until he had left before I stood up to follow, sticking the yellow jersey into my shorts so it wouldn't look like I was wearing a dress.

'Is she filling in for her husband?' I asked a tall boy beside me who said, 'Yeah,' and then he said his name was Steve. He said we were playing a crap team and it was only a friendly, so I'd be all right and he'd take the kick-outs if I didn't want to.

The manager of the other team was a guy called Mick and he was refereeing the game. Steve said it was just as well that Jenny didn't have to do it or we'd be playing hockey without sticks, and I laughed like I knew what he meant.

'We played them before lots of times and we always hockey them,' Steve said.

'Hey, you'll definitely hockey them now cos Jenny's your manager,' I said, and Steve laughed.

'Good one,' he said, stepping away to take up his position in the middle of the defence.

I stood on the goal-line and thought of the king at the start of a chess match. Maybe this was how he'd be feeling. He'd be watching his players line up to defend his position and hoping they'd be smart and strong enough to keep him safe from danger while they moved forward to destroy the enemy. Then I noticed that we had only ten on our team, but they had eleven and a lot more tall players.

The game started and the ball was up the other end of the pitch most of the time. I was watching Conor and he seemed to be spending all his time looking over at the touchline, but not always where his mother stood, shouting, and clapping her hands, and hopping like she was skipping with an invisible rope. It made me smile to look at how excited she was, even though it was a stupid friendly.

But Conor didn't seem a bit excited to be there. In fact, he looked miserable. It was like he was waiting for someone. About twenty minutes through the first half, he stopped playing altogether. Any time a high ball came near him he wouldn't jump to try and head it, and if someone shouted for a pass he just mouthed something back at them and kicked the ball away. After that nobody seemed to want to pass the ball to him. I could see his mother wasn't shouting any more. She was just standing there, watching her son and beginning to look as miserable as he did.

I let in only two goals in the first half. They were shots from far out, but they were way up too high in the goal for me to save. Steve said nobody would have saved them – not even Superman – but I knew he was just being nice. When the ref blew for half-time, I was too relieved to be worried about the score. Jenny came over to us with a bag of cut up oranges and bottles of water. She told us we were all bloody marvellous, but we all knew we weren't. Then Conor suddenly kicked over his bottle of water that was on the ground.

'We're crap!' he shouted and walked off the pitch towards the dressing room.

Jenny called after him, then followed him as far as the car park, and we could see the two of them arguing. She placed her hand on his shoulder like she was trying to coax him back but he just brushed it away and stalked off into the dressing room. Jenny stood there with her back to us and with her two hands raised to her head like she didn't know what to do next. A whistle blew and when we turned back to the pitch we could see Mick standing there waiting to get the second half started.

When he saw that we only had nine players, Mick gave us one of the lads from his own team and then he started the second half. I don't want to say too much about the score except that I lost count after three more goals flew past me. Steve said they weren't my fault. I felt like walking off too, long before it ended, but I knew it wouldn't be right to do that. And I felt sorry for Jenny. She was doing her best to cover for her husband while he was away doing whatever he was doing, and I thought Conor was scabby to have walked out on his teammates like that.

Jenny appeared back on the line shortly after the second half started, but there was no sign of Conor. She watched the game, but you could see her heart wasn't in it, cos every few minutes she'd look off towards the changing rooms, or towards the road, like as if she might spot Conor lurking there.

Then the game was over and Steve said, 'Well played!' and I said, 'Yeah!' and the two of us laughed.

After I changed back into my clothes, I sat listening to the boys giving out about the game and about Jenny. Steve said he was going to look for a different team to play for and everyone else agreed and said they were going to do the same. Nobody asked me what I was going to do.

'But won't Conor's da be upset if you all leave?' I asked Steve. 'Like, what's he going to say when he hears that?'

Steve stared at me like I was stupid.

'Conor's dad is dead. Did you not know that?'

'Dead!?'

'Yeah, he dropped down dead a couple of months ago. He just collapsed and died out in his garden. Conor was with him when it happened.'

'Jesus!'

'Yeah, and Jenny – she thought she could keep the team going, like for his sake, cos maybe that's what he would've wanted, but you saw what's after happening.'

I put my head down into my hands. Dead! The man in the photo – Conor's da. Dead! I couldn't believe how stupid I had been not to see it. I stared down at the kitbag and felt really bad that I still had it. And I hadn't brought the ball – or the photo!

'Hey, well done!' Jenny was there looking down at me and everyone else was gone. 'Sorry about Conor. He's still just very upset over his dad ... you heard about that?'

I nodded.

'And then his dad's lovely car was stolen with Conor's football jersey and other stuff that was special to him, in a bag exactly like your one there ... and we got news that they found the car burned out and I presume everything in it got burned because there was no sign of any of it.'

I stood up and wanted to tell her everything that had happened but I was afraid to. I lifted the bag off the floor. It felt really heavy now.

'Is Conor OK?'

'Thanks for asking, Kevin. You're the only one who did. But yeah, he walked home. It's not very far, so I gave him a key and let him go. And thanks for playing. I'm sorry but I don't think I'll need you again. I think my career as a manager is over before it even began.'

She let out a big long sigh and I felt really sorry for her.

She put out her hand and I shook it. It felt soft and warm, and she gave my hand a little squeeze before she let it go. She tried to smile but it had fake written all over it.

'Do you want me to give you a lift somewhere? I can drop you to a bus.'

'Can you drop me to your house, and I'll walk from there?'

'Oh. You know where I live?'

'Yeah,' I lied.

I put the kitbag into the back seat and sat in the front. The seats were soft creamy leather and the car smelled of Jenny's perfume. Neither of us spoke a word as we drove past the shopping centre, and onto a really quiet road that had loads of trees on it, and huge houses with long front gardens and driveways you could park a bus on.

She pulled into her driveway and it was all coloured pebbles and cobblelock – like Rory's, but lots more of it, and nicer, with different-coloured bricks making fancy designs. Someone had pulled a yellow hose down the side of the house and it lay coiled on the grass like a snake. The grass looked so green, like it was painted, and right in the middle of it were two tall trees like twins, all white and silvery from the way the sun was shining on them.

I got out of the car and said thanks and then went to walk away. But I'd only taken a few steps when she beeped at me. When I turned round she was getting out of the driver's seat and she had the kitbag in her hand.

'Hey, Kevin, you forgot your football gear.' Her smile was working again. 'I hope we weren't that bad that you don't ever want to see it again.'

I glanced at the bag and then I wasn't sure where to look.

'Maybe Conor would like it, cos it's ... you know ... Steve said he likes Man U. And that's cra– I mean, that was just terrible about the car, and I don't know if I am ever going to play football again.'

'Oh my gosh!' Jenny said and she handed me the bag and then put her arms around me and hugged me really tight.

'You're a little angel. Do you know that? A sweet little angel. Now go and get your bus. Conor will be all right. He just needs time.'

She was just about to start crying. I knew that look from Ma. So I took the bag, even though I wanted to tell her it wasn't mine. Then I turned and walked off. Before I went out her gate, I looked back and she was still standing there just watching me. I waved at her and she waved back, and then I ran hoping I'd find a bus stop nearby.

When I turned the corner out of Jenny's road I saw a car like Uncle Davy's turn into it. I stopped running and stared trying to see who was driving. It was Davy's car and Davy was at the wheel. Adam was in the front seat beside him. What were they doing going up towards Jenny's house? Then I remembered the black bag with all the stuff we found in the field. Davy was bringing it back at last. And he was probably doing it also to make up to Ma for being so narky about the chess set.

I walked slowly back towards Jenny's house and hid behind a car as I watched Davy pull in to the kerb across the road from the house. I waited for him or Adam to get out, but Conor suddenly appeared out onto the path in front of his house and began walking in my direction, so I turned and legged it for the bus.

8

Ma was in the sitting room asleep on the settee, with my *King and Castle* chess book open on her lap. *Friends* was on the telly.

Her phone buzzed on the table. I picked it up and saw the name: 'Sul'. I killed the sound and put the phone back where I found it. Ma opened her eyes.

'Was that my phone?'

'Yeah.'

'Who was it?'

'How would I know?'

She sat up suddenly and moved the book beside her onto the settee.

'Wait till I tell you, Kev. I went up to the community centre to see for myself what happened, and I spoke to Sul – I mean Mr Sullivan – and I think I might be after landing myself a job.'

'A job? In the community centre?'

'Can you believe it?'

'Ma, they're not going to give you a job after what happened.'

She took the phone off the table and smiled at the screen.

I watched her text a message. Why would Sully give her a job? Unless he thought Adam might leave the place alone if Ma was working there.

'So there won't be anyone here during the day?'

'Adam will be here. And I said it to your uncle.'

'You want Uncle Davy here – after what happened?'

'Yeah. I asked him if he could be around a bit more. Just until school starts back.'

'Ma, he doesn't want to be here any more. And you're hardly talking to him after what happened.'

'He's your uncle. He can do that much for you. Anyway you're fourteen, you're well able to mind yourself.'

Her phone pinged and her eyes got dragged back to the screen like it was a magnet.

'Well, I'm not checking in with him if I'm going somewhere.'

She smiled down at her message and then her thumb tapped an answer. She spoke as she tapped. 'I did ask could they hold off until school starts back but they need someone now.'

'And where am I supposed to go at lunch-time?'

She stopped tapping and looked at me.

'What do you mean?'

'When I'm back at school?'

'Then you can come over to the centre and I'll have lovely lunches made for you. And Rory might come with you.'

'Sure, Ma! You think he's gonna be allowed have lunch in the centre when his ma makes lunch for him at home?'

'OK. Well then, just bring along one of your other friends with you.'

I thought of Becky. Maybe I could ask her to join me. But I couldn't go there just me and Becky.

Ma lowered her eyes to her phone and seemed to be reading over what she wrote.

'Ma?'

'What?'

'How come you never ask me where I'm going?'

'What?' She pressed the send button and looked up at me.

'Why don't you ask me where I'm going when I go out?'

'But I do ask you, Kevin.'

'No you don't, Ma.'

'You're fourteen, Kevin, and sure you're in and out that door like a yo-yo. And anyway I know you're with Rory and I trust the two of you together.'

'Well, you never bring me anywhere. Like Rory's ma and da are always bringing him places.'

Ma put her phone in her pocket and still looked pleased with herself.

'Then I have news for you, Kevin. Me and you are going on a bit of a trip tomorrow. How would you like that?'

'Where?'

'I have tickets for a carnival.'

'The one near the Glen River Shopping Centre?'

'How do you know about that?'

'Rory's da said he might bring the two of us.'

'Well, now I'm bringing you instead.'

'I'll go if Rory can come with me.'

'Great. Why don't you ring him? The tickets I have are for tomorrow. We'll collect him on the way.'

'Collect him? You mean ... Davy's bringing us?'

Ma shook her head.

'No, Kevin. Your uncle is not bringing us.'

'Then who is?'

'Mr Sullivan.'

'Why is he bringing us?'

'He's scouting it out before he takes one of his groups. So me and you and Rory can help him with his field work.'

I left Ma and hurried up to my room and rang Rory. I told him about the boy Conor and the football match and then about Conor's da. Rory got such a shock he forgot he was supposed to be angry with me.

'Dead!?'

'Yeah. I knew the minute I saw him something was wrong.'

'Dead!'

'Yeah!'

'Then I bet you're glad you gave back all the football gear. Like, imagine how you'd feel if you hadn't.'

There was silence on the phone like he was gone.

'You did give it all back, Kevin. Didn't you?'

'Of course I gave it all back. I left it in the dressing room, didn't I?'

'You did the right thing, Kevin.'

I told him then about the trip and asked him if he'd like to come with us. He went off to ask his ma but when he came back he said he had something on and wouldn't be able to go with us. Like I said, his ma is a sap. But I didn't say it out loud, I just thought it.

The phone went suddenly silent again and I thought Rory had gone, but I saw it was my battery had died. I went up to my room to plug it in but my charger was gone. I went straight into Adam's room, even though he has a big poison sign stuck to his door that Ma just hates but wouldn't dare touch. My phone charger was plugged into the socket beside his bed. I unplugged it from the wall and then stopped in the middle of the room and looked around at all his stuff.

It always shocks me how tidy Adam keeps his room. It's like he's a girl, though I wouldn't ever say that to his face.

His bed was as neat-looking as a soldier's, with all his runners lined up in pairs on the carpet beneath the window. Ten pairs altogether.

I gazed now at his purple-coloured walls and at his black-and-white UFC poster with the 'GET YOUR KICKS' slogan on it in blood-red writing. Beside the poster was the drawing Adam did when he was in primary school and Ma liked so much she had it framed. It was a pencil drawing of a fancy convertible and Da was driving with Adam beside him and both of them wearing shades. Adam had put Ma in the back seat with her hair flying in the breeze so that her head looked like a hairdryer. And I was beside her, but you could only see the top of my head and it looked more like a spare wheel than a person.

I moved across the floor towards Adam's desk that Ma bought when he started secondary school. But Adam didn't last longer than two years in the place and left before they threw him out. The desk now held his laptop and games and the framed photo of Da and Davy leaning back against a red sports car and looking cool in their shades and white T-shirts. Surrounding the photo was Adam's prized collection of shot glasses and next to that was his wonky-looking bowl he'd made in some pottery class that was full to the brim with copper coins.

The stash of coins made me think of Adam's old hidey-hole that he used to have in his room. It was over near the radiator just beside the window. When they'd put in the radiator they had cut out a piece of floor board and hadn't nailed it back down. I went over to the rad and lifted up the edge of the carpet. Then I put my finger into a tiny hole where a knot had been in the wood and I lifted up the board.

I got a shock when I saw all the stuff that Adam had down in the hole. The binoculars from the car were there, as well as four ziplock plastic bags like Ma uses to freeze stuff, and there were old photos with a big red paperclip keeping them together.

I took out the photos and looked through them. The first one had four small square shots of Adam messing in a photo booth with some girl. He had his face lowered but I knew he was doing his crazy laugh. The girl with him was Madser's sister, Lizzy, and it looked like she was trying to give him a sloppy kiss. What was she doing with the likes of Adam? Everyone said she was really smart and was going to be starting in college, cos she'd done so well in her Leaving Cert. I shook my head in disbelief and shoved the photo to the back of the collection and examined the second one. It was one of Adam in his confirmation suit and a big smile like butter wouldn't melt in his mouth as Ma sometimes said.

I flicked through the rest of the photos. There were a few of Adam and Da and always a car in those photos as well. The last of the photos was of me and Adam visiting Santa Claus in some shopping centre. I was sitting on Santa's knee and looking scared. Adam had a big goofy smile on his face and was making rabbit ears over Santa's head with his two fingers.

I put the paperclip back on the photos and lifted out the first of the ziplock bags. I could see notes and coins through the plastic. It looked like Adam was using the hidey-hole instead of a bank. I was afraid to open the bag to count what he had but it looked like there were hundreds in it.

I lifted up a second bag and I could see it had a passport in it. I placed that bag back in the hole and took out the next one. It had tablets in it and other stuff that looked like herbs. But I knew from the whiff off it that it was Adam's stash of weed.

The last of the plastic bags was the heaviest. I opened the zip and looked inside. Whatever it was had been wrapped in layers and layers of cling film like the pieces of meat Ma froze in the freezer. I lifted it out, trying to figure out what it was. And then suddenly I knew.

A gun! Adam had a gun! The stupid thick was hiding a gun!

I could hear the front door opening downstairs and then a voice in the hall. I zipped the bag and stuffed it back in the hole exactly where I'd found it. I listened again. Adam's voice, talking to Uncle Davy, who sounded like he was waiting outside on the front step. I snapped the floorboard back in place and covered it with the carpet. Then I listened again. I could hear steps on the stairs – Adam's heavy steps – and then his voice.

'I'm getting it, I'm getting it!'

There wasn't time to get out of the room so I crawled underneath Adam's bed pushing empty kitbags and a sleeping bag out of the way. I tried to hardly breathe as the dust tickled my nose. Adam opened the door and went straight towards the window. I could hear the sound of the floorboard being lifted, then put back in place, then silence as if he was looking around the room to see if anyone had been in.

Davy called like he was in a hurry and I could hear Adam's feet go to the door and then lash down the stairs.

The front door banged shut and I waited for the sound of the car before I crawled out again. I went straight to the hidey-hole and looked inside to see what he had taken. The gun was still there. So were the other ziplock bags. It was the binoculars that were gone.

A gun! Now I wished I hadn't seen it. Maybe I should tell Davy. But what would he do? He'd want to get rid of it. But what if he got caught with it in his possession? Then he'd be the one in deep trouble.

I noticed I still had one of Adam's photos in my hand. It was the one with Santa. I looked towards the hidey-hole. The front door opened and Ma called my name. I stuck the photo in my pocket and examined the room to make sure I hadn't disturbed anything from the way Adam had left it.

'Come down into the kitchen,' Ma shouted up to me when I answered her from the landing.

She was kneeling down at the press below the sink, taking out her bottles of cleaning stuff and old J-cloths.

'There's something I want to show you,' she said.

'Ma, I'm not cleaning windows.'

She turned and smiled, and then showed me what else she had taken out from the press. It was a large plastic lunch box and I could hear something rattle inside. She reached in behind more cloths and bottles and pulled out the plastic chess board. She saw me staring at it and she laughed.

'It's the one hiding place I have in the house that I know nobody will ever look in.' When I didn't move, she laughed again. 'Adam took them out of the bin, so when you're finished playing with them, hide them in your room or just put them back in here.'

I gaped at Ma. 'Adam took them out?'

'Yeah. I think he got a shock with how Davy reacted.'

'Sure, Ma,' I said.

'What? You don't believe me?'

'Yeah, Ma. Of course I believe ya!'

'Well, it doesn't matter, does it, once you have them all back together again.'

I took the folded plastic board and smiled down at the container.

'And tomorrow we have that trip. Remember?'

'Rory can't go,' I said. 'He's ... he's not well.'

'Oh ... well then why don't you invite that little girl that called with the present?'

'She's not little, Ma.'

'You know what I mean. Just invite her.'

'And it wasn't a present. Jesus! It was just a spare set she'd left over.'

'OK, Kevin,' Ma said, and I could see the smile she was trying to hide. 'Why not invite her all the same?'

'She has a name, Ma!'

'Oh yeah, wasn't it something with a *y*. Ayla or Kaylie or something like that.'

'Ma, are you on something? I told you it's Becky. Her name's Becky.'

'There you go, it does have a *y*. And that's a lovely name. And she's a lovely girl.'

'Ma, you know who she is. She's Lunchbox's sister.'

'I'm just saying invite her along if Rory can't come.'

'I'm not inviting her.'

'Why not?'

'I'm just not. OK? And I'm not going either if Rory's not going.'

'You are going. I told Mr Sullivan you'd be there.'

'I'm not going to a carnival with just you and him.'

'You have to come, Kevin. You just have to.'

'Why?'

'Because I can hardly go with him on my own.'

'For God's sake, Ma. It's Sully! He's not going to jump on you.'

9

Ma wore her denim jacket with a black V-necked T-shirt underneath it. She wasn't wearing her gold chain with the rings but had a silver one on instead, with what looked like a glassy red letter R framed in a tiny square of silver. When I asked her what it was she said Sully made it for her. She said he made little bits of jewellery on the side and was thinking of taking a stall in the Wednesday market. Ma said he'd promised to teach her how to make stuff if she was interested. I told her I preferred the gold chain with the rings but she said she needed to be able to wear different things to match her mood – whatever that meant.

Sully was sitting in his car outside the community centre and he got out as soon as he spied us walking towards him. He looked completely different. He had trimmed his beard so tight it looked like a shadow on his face. There was a shine above his forehead where he had cut his little nest of wispy hairs as if to show off where he was going bald. The rest of his long black hair was tied up in a pony-tail.

And Sully wasn't wearing one of his usual T-shirts either, but had a white shirt on that had black buttons in a line down the front, with a black pocket on it and no collar. And instead of his denim jacket he was wearing a blue woolly one that I'd never seen before. He wore his usual jeans, though, with a pair of runners instead of his boots. Ma gave me a nudge in the back with her elbow, cos she knew I was staring. He smiled at Ma as soon as we reached the car.

'You scrub up well,' Ma said, laughing. 'We hardly recognised you. Isn't that right, Kevin?'

'Yeah,' I said.

'Thanks for the compliment, Blondie,' Sully said and laughed.

Ma's face went scarlet.

'You used to have blonde hair, Ma?'

'Yeah, out of a bottle.'

'When I used to play in that band I had she was in the front row of all of our gigs, herself and her sister, Rita.'

'That's because Rita fancied you,' Ma said.

'And there was me hoping it was you,' Sully said.

Ma ducked into the front seat of the car. I climbed in the back, and sat right behind the driver's seat so Sully couldn't see me in the mirror. He drove an old Honda Civic. It was the kind of car that Adam and Madser liked to drive but I kept that info to myself.

'Thanks for doing this for me, Kevin,' Sully said.

Ma put her hand back and patted me on the leg like I was a child.

'Isn't this nice, Kevin? A day out for the two of us! I can't remember the last time the two of us had a day out together.'

'Would you like me to play some music?' Sully asked.

Ma looked back at me to let me know he was asking me the question.

'His band used to play Beatles songs. Did you know that?'

I shook my head.

'Remember all the times I used to sing to you, Kevin? "We all live in a yellow submarine." Except we used to change it to "We all live on smelly margarine."'

Ma and Sully laughed and then they started talking about her new job and holidays and other boring stuff. I thought of the poster for the Freak Out ride I'd seen – which was the only reason I'd said I'd go with them. Then I thought of my own freak out and Rory with his black eye.

'Will you ever forget the place in Wexford?'

Ma turned round this time to let me know she was talking to me.

'Wexford?'

'Remember? What was it called – the something twist?'

She started to laugh and suddenly it all came back to me.

It happened when I was ten or so and Adam was about fourteen – around the time when he began to turn mean.

We were on a week's holiday in a mobile home in Wexford that had a beach and a funfair and not much else. Ma had been invited down by Rita, who got the loan of the place for practically nothing from this woman she worked with on the tills in Dunnes.

It was a really sunny evening and Ma and Rita were lashing into red wine out on the deck at the front of the mobile home. And the two of them were talking really loud and cackling like witches and I wanted to go to the funfair but Ma wouldn't let me go on my own. She asked Adam to bring me. But Adam was in a huge huff, cos he didn't want to be down in Wexford at all, especially cos Ma wouldn't let Madser come, and she wouldn't let him stay on his own at home either. In the end, Ma could get him to bring me only by giving him a load of extra money.

When we got down to the funfair, Adam put me into a bumper car with him, but he wouldn't let me drive. Three times we went around and I said I was going back to tell Ma that he was being mean. He told me to shut up or he'd keep all the money for himself and then he dragged me off to a big waltzer. Adam was hoping I'd hate it and it might make me sick so he could bring me home early, but I loved it. He wouldn't let me go on it a second time. He said it was babyish and I should go on faster stuff. So he took me to the chair-o-planes and I loved that too and he was raging. So he said I should try out the Sizzler Twist.

'The Sizzler Twist, Ma!' I said. 'That's what it was called.'

'Yeah,' Ma said, laughing. 'The Sizzler Twist.'

'I had to bring him home, Ma – and him saying it was food poisoning.'

Ma turned around and laughed out loud.

'Don't remind me, Kevin. I had to throw out his track-suit, it was so manky.'

'This one we're going to has a Freak Out,' Sully said suddenly.

'Yeah,' I said, like it was the most boring thing in the world.

The Freak Out was a huge monster of a swinging arm that had four claw-like hands coming out the end of it and I couldn't wait to have a go on it.

'Almost there,' Sully said, and I slipped down in the seat when I saw we were passing the turn to Conor's road. I thought of the football gear and I knew I'd have to return it soon before Rory came back on the scene. I checked my pocket but I only had the photo from Adam's room. Then I thought of the gun. Ma wouldn't be laughing if she knew about that. I would have to tell Davy. Davy would know what to do and how to get rid of it. But I tried not to think about it. I'd think about it later when I got back home.

Sully reversed into a parking space and we all got out and gazed up and around at all the rainbow colours, and listened to the noise of the generators mixed with carnival music and shouts and screams coming from far away at the other side. It looked brilliant. It sounded even better. And Ma was smiling, and when I looked at her she tossed my hair with her fingers.

'Hey, don't start that, Ma,' I said, smoothing it back into place.

There was a giant Ferris wheel in the distance and we would work our way towards it. That was my plan anyway. Sully went off to talk to a man at the entrance gate about the price of tickets for his planned visit with his group.

'You stay with me and Mr Sullivan,' Ma said like she could read my thoughts.

'Ma! Will you call him Sully?'

'All right, but stay with me. And we'll try and go on everything together, me and you.'

'What about ... him?'

Ma laughed and looked over towards Sully as he headed back towards us.

'He won't leave the ground. Won't even go upstairs on a bus!'

The front of the carnival had the little kiddy rides, a candyfloss stall and a shop selling sweets, Slush Puppies, ice cream cones and popcorn. And there was a van selling chips that I'd check out later.

I put my hand in my pocket and felt Davy's money. And I had another tenner that I found on my bedside locker. It was just sitting there and I thought Ma had given it to me. But Ma said she hadn't put it there. She said that left Adam or the tooth fairy.

'You're the tooth fairy,' I said to Ma, but she only laughed and said, 'Not this time.'

We went for the bumper cars first. Watching them made me smile cos they looked like giant shoes that had thick flat rubber soles. Some of the drivers were really good but most of them were crap. There was one girl and she was going round like a dog trying to bite its own tail. There was another kid and you could see he was just spending his time trying to avoid being hit and he wasn't bothered trying to hit anyone else. I didn't see the point of driving like that.

The cars stopped and emptied and I ran for the nearest one. Ma got into one also, and after they were all filled the ceiling buzzed and sparked and we moved off and around. Someone bumped into the back of me and only for the seat belt I would have shot out the front like a bullet. When I turned round, I saw Sully with a big evil grin on his face and then he swerved away. I chased after him and then *WHAM!* I got hit again except this time it was Ma doing her mad cackle of a laugh. I couldn't believe it! They were ganging up on me.

We stayed in the bumpers for a second buzz around and when we stood out, me and Sully teased Ma about her driving.

'Just as well you don't have a car!' Sully said, laughing.

We headed for the waltzers after that, and I sat with Ma just to please her while Sully waved whenever we passed by him. Then I headed straight for the Freak Out.

'You're not going on that?' Sully said when he caught sight of the monstrous metal arm with all the bucket seats clenched in its fist.

I looked at Ma and she smiled.

'After you,' she said, putting on a posh voice, and we paid our money and sat beside each other, with pads and straps locking us in place.

'I don't know about this,' Ma said in a shaky voice like she was suddenly frightened. Her fingers sought out the chain around her neck but she quickly let it go when she realised she wasn't wearing the one with the rings on it. *Serves her right*, I thought. And it was too late for her to get out. We were in the grip of the giant's huge fist and he was going to have some fun with us before putting us back down to earth again.

'I'm really not sure about this,' Ma cried again as we started slowly spinning. Then the pace increased and the screams came with it, and the earth was no longer below but above us, and then to one side, and then the other. I screamed my guts out and I wasn't sure if Ma was scream-ing or crying. But it was all over too soon as the giant arm slowed down and the little fists we sat in stopped spinning and then came to a halt.

'Ma! That was deadly!' I shouted when I saw her scram-bling to get out of her seat. 'Can we go again?'

But Ma wasn't listening to me, and Sully had to dart forward and grab her before she collapsed at our feet.

'Ma, are you all right?' I shouted, trying to hold her up with Sully.

'I don't ... feel ... good ...' she groaned. 'I don't feel ... good ... oh Jesus what was I thinking? Oh gawwwd!'

Sully helped her step away from the Freak Out and I could see everyone staring at her and smiling. But it wasn't that funny.

Sully helped her walk to a bench near the grassed area and there were two girls sitting there, but when they saw her face, they scattered like she had some sort of killer disease. Her head had fallen onto her chest and she was groaning. Bits of her hair were plastered to the corner of her mouth.

'Are you all right, Ma?' I asked, leaning in to try and see her face.

Sully tried to put his arm around her to comfort her but she pushed it away.

'NOOO!' she shrieked. 'Nobody come near me!'

She looked up then and blinked like the sun was in her eyes. 'Oh, Kevin – if everything would only stop spinning!'

'Are you all right?' Sully asked me.

'Yeah!' I said, insulted.

'I thought I was going to die,' Ma said. 'I honestly thought I was going to die. I wanted to die.'

Sully laughed at that – the way she said it, like he believed her – and I started to laugh too. Sully put his hand on her shoulder and this time she let him leave it there. Ma looked up at me and her eyes didn't look as scared-looking. 'You go off, Kevin. You go off on your own for half an hour or so ...'

I looked at Sully.

'I'll mind your mother, Kevin. We'll text you when we're ready to go.'

I looked at Ma.

'Go on. Text us if you need anything.'

'OK,' I said, trying not to seem too pleased with myself.

I headed straight for the shop and bought a chocolate doughnut and a can of Coke. Then I wandered through the carnival, letting my feet take me wherever they wanted to go. I stopped at a stall that had a line of basketball nets on its back wall. It was run by a tall skinny man with grey hair tied back in a ponytail and a thick grey moustache.

I was never really much good at basketball so I let my feet take me back towards the bumper cars. I watched them bump and screech, but I didn't make a run for any of the empty seats cos it's never much fun in them when you don't have anyone to chase after. I finished the doughnut and licked bits of melted chocolate off my fingers and then moved farther into the carnival, towards where I could hear loud girly screams. They were coming from the Wave Swinger, a chair-o-plane ride with a tilting top. Everyone was trapped in their seats as they were swung in dizzy circles through the sky. The sun was getting hotter so I took my jacket off. I stood and drank the Coke and watched them get dizzier and wished Rory was with me.

As I was looking up, I saw something fall off one of the chairs and it seemed to be heading for me like someone had thrown it at me. I held my jacket up to try and protect myself and what happened was that whatever fell landed in the jacket.

I lowered the jacket and looked at what I'd caught. It was a phone – a new iPhone that must have fallen from someone's pocket. I looked around. No one was looking in my direction. I was going to shove the phone in my pocket. Then I thought that was something Adam would do. So I waited for the ride to finish to see who would come looking for it. The chairs swooped round like a flock of birds, then slowed and stopped and everyone unbuckled their belts and jumped clear.

Four boys came down off the steps and headed for where I was standing. I couldn't believe it when I saw that the boy out in front of the other three was Conor. He had his eyes lowered, searching the path and the grassed area for something. I stepped back behind a sign and watched the other three search with him. They were three of the lads from the team but I couldn't remember any of their names.

'It'll be in bits, Conor,' the tallest boy said like he was already fed up looking.

'I know,' Conor said. 'But I just want to find it, to show Mum.'

'I told you it was going to fall out,' one of the other boys said, but Conor wasn't really listening to him. He was heading back towards the Wave Swinger. He stopped and looked at the three lads who had given up the search. They were looking at their own phones like they were checking for texts or something.

'Hey, help me find it, will ye? Please!'

'I told you, Conor. It'll be in bits so there's not much point.'

Then the two other boys walked off and left Conor and the tall boy on their own.

'Please, Gar, please! Help me find it.'

The one called Gar shrugged.

'It's gone, Conor. OK?' He turned and walked off quickly after his two mates.

Conor opened his mouth to shout something after them but then closed it again and continued his search. He moved in closer to the Wave Swinger. I could see the man who operated it come over to him. I could see Conor point to his pocket and then look up at the dangling chairs as he tried to explain what he was doing. Then he saw a rubbish bin and he darted over to it and started to empty paper and cans out of it. The man came over and gave out to him and made him put all the stuff back in again. The man pointed at an exit sign and I could see he was getting narkier by the second. Conor turned his back on him and walked towards me like he'd given up on his phone. I could see from the way he was hurrying with his head down that he was upset.

'Hey!' I called. But he didn't hear me. I ran after him and tapped him on the shoulder. 'Hey!' I said again.

He turned round like he was in a daze. I could see the big frown on his face like he was trying to remember where he had seen me before.

'The football match! Ten–nil.'

'Oh yeah,' he said, then turned away again.

'Don't you want it, then?'

He turned round once more.

'What?'

I showed him the phone. He just stared at it like it was a bar of chocolate or something.

'It's your phone. It fell out of your pocket when you were on the Wave Swinger.'

Now he was staring at me, his eyes wide and his mouth open.

'It can't be. It would've broken!'

'I caught it.'

'In your hands?'

'Yeah, I had to, or it would've hit me on the head.'

I didn't say anything about using my jacket. He stared at the phone, still not believing it was his. He gazed back towards the Wave Swinger like he was trying to do some sort of mental maths calculation.

'No way! You couldn't have caught it.'

He looked me in the face, then cautiously lifted the phone off my palm and studied it. He pressed buttons and when he saw the face of it light up, his own face lit up too and I thought of the photo of him and his da outside Old Trafford.

'I can't believe you caught it!' he said, his voice full of wonder. 'That was like a miracle.'

'I'm a goalie, amn't I!'

He smiled at me, pressing more buttons, then he turned the phone over in his hands like he was searching for cracks or something.

'Hey, I'm sure your ma would've bought you a new one.'

'Yeah, but my dad bought me this one So it's special. And it has photos and ... stuff.'

'Like Man– I mean, your da's matches?'

'Yeah,' he said. He slipped the phone deep into his jacket pocket.

'Do you want to go on any of the rides?' I didn't mean to ask him but it just came out.

He looked off back to where his mates had gone. 'OK. But I don't think I've any money left.'

'I've plenty,' I said.

Conor followed me as I headed back towards the Freak Out. He stopped, though, like his feet were stuck, when he saw where I wanted to go.

'Hey, I don't know if I want to go on that.'

'You have to go on it. It's deadly. It's just the best ride in the park.'

He eyed the ride as if it was some sort of dangerous animal – like I was asking him to climb up on top of a camel or something.

'I wouldn't go on it for the lads, and they were teasing me.'

'Don't mind them. I want you to go, cos there's no fun if I have to go on my own.'

'I don't know. I'm afraid I might ... get sick.'

'Did you get sick on the chair-o-planes? Or on anything else?'

'No.'

'So you won't get sick on this, I promise. Anyway, you have to do it with me. I found your phone, didn't I? And you know what that means?'

He shook his head and frowned.

'It means that once you're with me, nothing bad can happen to you. I'm like ... I'm like ... one of those guardian angels that suddenly appear out of the blue.

Conor looked at me like I was maybe losing it. Then he smiled so I took that as a yes. I paid for the two of us and spoke to him as he got buckled into his seat. 'It's good for you, this, cos you can just scream your head off when it starts to get scary.'

The machine made a sudden jerk to warn us it was ready to start and I could see Conor's face all tensed up like he wanted to say he'd changed his mind. But it was too late for that now.

'Hey, I'm right beside you, so nothing can go wrong,' I said.

The metal fist took both of us in its grip and began to twirl and swirl us gently. Then faster and faster it went and suddenly the monster began to swing his arm, and earth and sky swapped places again, backwards and forwards, upwards and downwards, all the time spinning us like we were in the belly of a tumble dryer. I let loose a huge cry like I was trying to empty my throat of all sound. When the ride finished and I turned to Conor, his eyes looked like they'd grown bigger in his head.

'Do you want to go again?' I shouted.

'No way,' he said. Then he laughed. It was the first time I'd heard him laugh since I'd met him.

When we turned to step down off the ride we saw Conor's three mates with bags of chips in their hands and all three staring up at him with their mouths open.

'You went on that?' Tall Boy cried.

'Yeah!' Conor said. 'It was deadly!'

He took his phone out of his pocket.

'And look!'

He showed them the phone.

'No way!' the three boys shouted like they were one.

'Kevin caught it!'

'No way!' the three of them cried again.

'Hey, I'm a goalie!'

Then they all laughed like they remembered the football match and the final score.

The smallest boy held out his chips towards Conor and Conor took a few. He pointed the bag at me but I shook my head. I suddenly realised how hungry I was and that I needed to get chips of my own.

'Do you want to come round the rest of the rides with us?' Tall Boy asked me.

'No. I have to go now.' I nodded at Conor. 'See ya!' I said and then I walked back towards the entrance, knowing they were watching me.

As I was waiting for the chips I looked back towards the Freak Out. The boys were gone. I was just about to look away when I saw Adam come up through the crowds of people. Davy was walking behind him and talking to someone. When they got closer I could see it was the man from the basketball stall he was talking to. Adam was carrying two paper cups of coffee and he had a plastic bag dangling from his wrist that looked like it had sandwiches in it. Davy and the man stopped and Adam stopped also to wait for them. Davy took the man's hand and shook it and then they hugged like they were the best of buddies. The man turned then and went back in the direction of his stall and Davy and Adam came walking towards where I was queuing. I turned my head away so they wouldn't spot me, and when I turned back to look for them, I could see them heading for the exit.

I wondered what they'd been doing in the carnival. Maybe Davy was meeting the man because he hoped he might give Adam a real job for a while. Or maybe he was looking for some sort of work for himself that would get him away from his job in Deegan's garage. Ma didn't like Deegan so maybe he hoped a new job would impress Ma and make her like him more. Or maybe they were just trying to sell him something. My phone beeped and put an end to all my thoughts about Davy and Adam. It was Ma sending me a text wondering where I was.

10

'No way!' Rory shouted. 'No way!' We were in his da's shed and I didn't know whether he was amazed cos I'd just taken his knight or because I'd caught Conor's phone. 'I can't believe you caught his phone – just like that!'

'It was no big deal. Why is everyone surprised I caught his phone? I am the greatest goalie in the world.'

Rory laughed. 'Yeah, the world must have shrunk.'

He stared at his other black knight and I could see him thinking about his next move.

'Snookered!' I said.

'You can't get snookered in chess, Kev.'

'That's what you think.'

He bent his head over his army and went to move a piece, then changed his mind.

'Touch-move!' I said.

'I know. I didn't touch it.'

'And Conor got on the Freak Out with me. He was afraid at first but I persuaded him. And he asked me to call for him.'

Rory looked up from the chess board.

'What? He asked you to call for him. Like ... to hang out?'

'Yeah, I suppose so.'

'And what did you say?'

'I said I would.'

'What! Are you crazy, Kevin?'

'And why wouldn't I call?'

'Because your brother stole his da's car and you took his football gear. What's he going to say if he finds out about that?'

'He's not going to find out. Like, I'm not calling to tell him, am I? I just want to call ... I dunno ... just to see.'

'What?'

'I dunno, Rory. I'm just curious, that's all.'

'Curious?'

'Yeah.'

'So when are you calling over to him?'

'Today.'

'Today?'

'Yeah. I'm going there now as soon as I beat you. And you can come with me.'

'I can't.'

'Oh yeah, I forgot! You have to get a visa from your ma before you can go anywhere.'

'Not funny, Kevin.'

'Yeah, well I don't need a visa cos Ma started her job today, so I'll be back before she gets home.'

(Ma had gone off in the morning, giddy and nervous like a child starting her first day in school. She rang after half an hour to see if Davy was around and I said he was downstairs even though he wasn't.)

'And don't go near the community centre,' I warned Rory.

'Why?'

'Cos Ma's working at the deli counter down there, and I'm supposed to be hanging round with you until she comes back.'

'OK.'

Rory's face suddenly lit up with a huge smile and he slid his black queen across the width of the board.

'Check!' he said, and laughed as he sat back on his stool.

I stared at the board. He leaned in over it once more like he'd found a new discovery, and a big evil grin creased his face.

'Checkmate!'

'Feck's sake, how did that happen?'

Rory laughed again.

'You took your eye off the ball.'

'We don't have balls in chess.'

'Yeah, Kev. Just a balls-up. That must be ten–nil to me at this stage.'

'You feck off, Rory. For that you can lend me your bike.'

'What?'

'Your bike. I can get over to Conor's faster that way through the park and the estates.'

'My da said I'm not to lend it to anyone, Kev.'

'I'm not anyone, Rory. And look, I'll have it back in an hour.'

Rory frowned like he didn't believe me.

'I'm leaving the chess set here with you, amn't I?' I said. 'I'm trusting you to mind that, amn't I?'

'OK, Kev, and if you fall off it you get back up on it straight away.'

'What?'

'That's what Sully says, if you fall off your bike you have to get back up on it straight away or you'll never cycle again.'

'But Sully doesn't even own a bike,' I said, laughing.

'Yeah, I know. But you make sure you don't fall off it. And when you come back bring it straight here. Don't leave it at your own house.'

I knew what he was getting at, but I didn't say anything. I was just glad that we were friends again and I was in his shed, if not in his house.

'I'm just calling to see him, Rory, cos I feel a bit sorry for him ... after what happened.'

'Yeah, I know, Kev. But you'd want to be careful. Like, you don't want him to ever find out about Adam and his da's car, and that it was you who took his football gear.'

'I'm giving it back to him, amn't I?'

Rory stared at me.

'I've given it back to him, I mean ... except for the ball. OK?'

'Kevin, you have to give everything back! You have to.'

'I know,' I said, knocking over my king.

11

The yellow hose was still coiled like a snake on the grass, and the Beemer was parked in the driveway. I pressed the bell beside the black door but nothing happened. I pressed it a second time, but again there was no sound. The door knocker was a big lion's paw. I lifted it and rapped the door with it. I could hear steps inside and then the door half opened and Jenny's face peered out at me. She had her mobile pressed to her ear and she frowned at me like I was some sort of nuisance caller. Then her eyes widened and her mouth fell open like she suddenly realised who I was.

'Call you back!' she said into the phone before lowering it to her side.

'Kevin!' She shouted my name like I was the prodigal son come home, and then she pulled me towards her and gave me a huge hug that nearly smothered me. 'Oh, it's so great to see you, Kevin. Conor told me all about you catching his phone. I don't know how you did it. You're ... you're just a wonder.'

'I'm a goalie,' I said, getting sick of the joke.

'Well, I think you're the best goalie in the world.'

She turned around and shouted Conor's name up the stairs. 'I'm so glad you called for him. He's spending too much time on those computer games. It's not good for him.'

She shouted Conor's name a second time and he appeared at the top of the landing and peered out over the banisters at me.

'Look who's called by. It's Kevin.'

He stepped quickly down the stairs and nodded and smiled like he was glad to see me. He was wearing a white T-shirt and jazzy-looking shorts with zig-zag lines on them and a pair of flip-flops on his bare feet.

Jenny frowned down at her phone like she'd forgotten who she was talking to.

'I'll be in the study, Conor, if you need me for anything. And don't forget what we decided, you'll be with Grandad tomorrow.'

'What *you* decided, Mum!'

'Not now, Conor. OK?'

'What does she do, your mother?' I asked when she was gone. I could hear her now on her mobile from the other side of the closed door.

'She's a bank manager. She has the day off today but she might as well be still at work. She's been on her phone all morning and then she gives out to me for being on the computer.'

'And what did your da do – like, besides train you at football?'

'My dad? He was a lecturer. Business studies.'

I looked down the length of the hallway. It was bigger than our kitchen.

'Hey, your house is like a palace.'

Conor laughed.

'Would Sir like a tour?' he said in a posh voice.

'Yeah, deadly! But I can't pay you anything.'

'That's all right. Sir has paid me already with his great saves.'

The two of us burst out laughing at that. He was better even than Ma or Rory at putting on a posh voice.

'Follow me, if you'll be so kind.' He bowed and flip-flopped down the wooden floor. I followed after him down the long hallway past a tall mirror and a hat-stand and found myself in the kitchen that looked nearly as big as the bottom of our whole house.

'WOW!' I cried when I saw the floor. It was covered in huge black and white tiles. 'Hey, you could play chess on that.'

'The floor?'

'Yeah! All you'd need are those big giant chess pieces like I saw outside a hotel in Wexford.'

'Hey, I know that hotel! We stayed there once. Did you stay there?'

'No. Ma had to use the toilet.'

Conor burst out laughing and stood inside the kitchen door waiting for me to finish staring at stuff. And I was staring. If Ma had been with me, she would have given me a right thump.

There was an enormous wooden table in the middle of the kitchen with eight chairs – eight! – around it, and a big vase of flowers like a colour explosion in the centre of the table. Four lights hung down from the ceiling over the table like silver and black space ships. There was a huge dresser at the end of one wall with a long black couch beside it. Another wall was like a gallery full of family photos and Conor seemed to be in most of them. Conor's da and Jenny were in a lot of them also.

'You've no brothers or sisters then?' I asked him.

'No. What about you?'

'No. No, I don't,' I said.

'Hey, sounds like you're not sure.'

'Hey, is that your da?' I asked even though I knew it was.

'Yeah, at my confirmation,' Conor said.

'Did you make much money?'

'Over a grand. What about you?'

'About four hundred.'

'Did your da sponsor you?'

'Yeah,' I said even though it was Uncle Davy who had stood with me. I don't know why I didn't tell him that my da had also died. I just didn't feel like talking about it because it would have made me think about Ma crying that morning of the confirmation cos Davy had just come back into our lives. I didn't know if her tears were because she was sad or happy. Or maybe she was both. And Rita and Davy were upset too and Adam had to tell them all to get a grip or they'd ruin the day on me.

I looked around at the rest of the kitchen. They had an island with stools like Rory had, but this one was bigger and classier. The stools had arms on them made of silver and black leather.

'Hey, did they make *Star Trek* in here?' I asked.

'Can you imagine? My mum could have been Uhura.'

'Yeah,' I said. 'But they'd have to call her Yahoorya cos she's Irish.'

Conor burst out laughing like it was the funniest joke he'd ever heard. I couldn't believe he hadn't heard it before cos me and Rory spent a whole week saying it after seeing the *Star Trek* film she was in.

I moved over to the sink and looked past it and out towards their back garden.

'You've a sunroom?'

'Our conservatory,' Conor said, but then sighed like he had suddenly got bored with showing me around.

He walked out the door of the kitchen into another passageway and then it seemed like we were in a smaller kitchen that had a washing machine and a dryer and loads of clothes piled in a heap on the floor.

'That's handy,' I said. 'You've two kitchens.'

'This is the scullery,' Conor said. 'Well, that's what my nan used to call it.'

I was going to ask where she was but then I didn't cos I was afraid she might be dead too.

'A scullery?'

'Yeah.'

'Hey, how come I don't see any?'

'What?'

'Skulls.'

'Very funny,' Conor said, but he didn't laugh.

I poked my head inside another door and saw a room that was all tiles from floor to walls with a shower hanging down from the ceiling like it was a lamp.

'Wow!' I said.

'That's our wet room. Have you never seen one before?'

'Yeah, in my house. But only when it rains.'

Conor made a smile.

'Do the football team come back here then?'

'Yeah,' Conor said and gave a short laugh as he closed the door and continued with the tour that still hadn't reached the sunroom. The next room I poked my head into was a small storeroom full of blankets, sheets, raincoats and stuff like that.

'Hey, it must be very easy here to hide from your ma,' I said.

'We used to play hide and seek when I was small, at birthday parties. Dad used to get us to play it like when you found the person, you had to hide with them. He called it "sardines".'

There were no more doors to search behind except the

ones to the garden and to the sunroom. I wanted to see the sunroom first and when I followed him in there I saw leather couches and woolly rugs on a wooden floor.

'I really could live in this house,' I said.

'My mum says it's too big now. Like ...'

'Yeah.'

'I'll show you the garden,' he said, and walked past me towards a patio door that led out onto a large area of decking. There were four wooden garden chairs around a table that was tiled on top. Off to the side near the wall was what looked like a stall from the carnival. It had a counter in front and a closed plastic curtain above it that had pictures of lemons on it.

'Did you steal that from the carnival?' I said.

Conor looked where I was pointing.

'That? It's just a bar. Dad liked ...'

'Deadly,' I said, turning away from it to gaze down the long garden.

Right beside the decking was a trampoline – big enough for four or five people to go on at a time. Beyond that was a square of long grass that had a pond with a net over it and a twirly clothes line with no clothes on it that looked like a giant version of one of Ma's cocktail glasses. Beyond that was more grass and white plastic goalposts bent out of shape with a net thrown over them. Behind that were more silvery trees that went back towards a fancy concrete shed that had a big leafy plant climbing all over it. Across from the shed was this weird plastic hut like a large see-through igloo.

'What's that?' I asked, pointing to the plastic.

Conor turned his gaze to follow where I was pointing. 'That's Dad's tunnel.'

'A tunnel! Where's he trying to go? Australia?' Then I remembered. 'Sorry,' I said.

'He liked to grow things in there.'

'Can I see what's in it?'

'It's boring,' he said and turned away from it. He went and sat on one of the garden chairs. I peered beyond the tunnel and the shed to the brick wall at the very end of the garden which had a green wooden door in the middle of it.

'What's out beyond the door?'

'It's just a lane that nobody uses any more. And beyond that there's just a playing pitch that belongs to the school.'

'You should cut your grass and fix that goal. It's deadly.'

Conor got up from his seat and the two of us looked down towards the white plastic posts and the squares of netting.

'Mum said she'll have to get someone in now to manage it. Dad loved being out here. He planted all those trees and got the tunnel in.'

The two of us went silent. I put my hand in my back pocket and felt the little wallet that had the photo of Conor's da in it. Now I was glad I'd brought it with me.

'When I'm out here, I sometimes feel like someone is watching me,' he said.

'There's a lane out there, so you could have a Peeping Tom?' I said.

'No. I don't mean like that. Like ... like there's some-one ...'

He pointed up towards the sky. 'Like someone up there.'

'Your da, you mean.'

'Yeah. I just get the feeling that he's looking after me. And I was thinking about what you said.'

'What did I say?'

'About you being like a guardian angel.'

'Hey, I was only joking.'

'I know you were. But it's just ... it felt good when you caught the phone. Like that was spooky. Like you just caught it and you didn't know whose phone it was and it just happened to be mine ... and I would have been really upset if I'd lost it. And then remember you turned up to help us with the football match.'

'Some help. Ten–nil!'

'Yeah, but if you hadn't come, I would've had to go in goal just to please my mum.'

'I suppose so,' I said.

'Would you like a drink?'

I turned to look at the bar. Conor laughed. 'No! Not from there. From the fridge.'

'Go on! I'm gasping.'

He walked back the way we'd come and I followed him into the kitchen. The fridge was in a corner of the room and nearly as tall as the ceiling. I knew it was called an American fridge because Ma showed me a photo of one from one of her magazines. It was the type of fridge she said she'd buy when she won the lotto. This one was bright red and had an ice-maker at the front of it. Conor opened the door and took out two Cokes. He handed one to me and then went to sit on one of the stools at the island. He twirled on the stool like it was something in a kiddies' playground and I examined all the stuff that was stuck to the fridge door. They were magnets of all sorts of different places, and faces, and strange names.

'Hey, were you in all these places?'

Conor placed a foot on the floor to stop the stool from moving and glanced at the fridge door.

'I was in some of them, but my mum and dad do a lot of travel – I mean, they did. It was to do with their work. So they bring those – *brought* those back.'

He drank from his Coke can and started twirling on his seat again. Then he stopped and lowered his head and went really still like he was remembering something. The magnets were really cool-looking. There was a red devil holding a large fork in his hand and I knew where he had picked that one up. There was a New York yellow taxi one and another one with a gondola. There was a windmill that I knew had to be from Holland and a black bull stuck to the Spanish flag. I looked over at Conor and he was rubbing his eyes. I put my hand in my back pocket and took out the little wallet and I let it fall on the floor at my feet. Then I pushed it in towards the bottom of the fridge so only a little piece of it was sticking out.

'Hey! Conor!' He didn't seem to hear me so I called him again.

'Hey, I think one of your magnets is under your fridge.' I bent down and pulled it out and held it in front of my face. 'I don't think it's a magnet though. It has the Man U crest on it.'

'Hey,' Conor cried, jumping off the stool.

I handed him the wallet and he stared at it like it was treasure.

'What? What is it?'

He opened the wallet and pulled out the photo and gazed at it.

'What?'

'It's the little wallet I bought in the Mega Store at Old Trafford. I put a photo of me and Dad in it. Look.'

I peered real close at it, like I was seeing it for the first time.

'Cool.'

'Yeah! I thought I'd lost it with all the other stuff.'

'What other stuff?'

'The stuff in the car.'

'Oh yeah! Your ma told me about your da's car.'

He put the photo back inside the wallet.

'See, Kevin. See what I mean?'

'What?'

'It's like ... good stuff happens when you're around. Hey, wait till I tell my mum. She'll be thrilled because this was her favourite one from the Old Trafford trip.'

'You mean she went with you?'

'It was her that took the photo.'

I emptied the Coke can and burped. 'I'm glad I brought that up!' I put the can down on the black marble worktop. 'Hey, I've to go,' I said.

'But you'll come back.'

'Yeah, sure.'

'Thanks, Kevin.'

'Hey, I'm a goalie. I save the day.'

Conor laughed and then headed out the kitchen door in search of his mother. I followed after him, not really wanting to talk to her or listen to him tell her about how I found the wallet. I could hear her on the phone in her room as I passed the door. It sounded like she was giving out to someone. Conor hesitated at the door before opening it.

'Hey, Kevin. What's your second name?'

'My second name?'

'Yeah, cos we can be friends on Facebook.'

I thought of my Facebook page and I wasn't sure if it was a good idea for him to be reading it and knowing more about me, especially cos I still had all his football gear.

'Did I not tell you?' I said.

'No.'

'Well, that's cos I don't have a second name.'

'What?' Now he had a grin on his face but his eyes looked a little bit unsure.

'Yeah, angels don't have second names. So I'm just – Kevin.'

Conor laughed.

'Kevin Angel,' he said.

'Yeah. That's me.'

'OK, I'll just have to get it off you the next time you're here,' he said, turning the door handle to go and tell his mother about his latest find. Once he was inside, I headed for the front door and Rory's bike.

12

We were in the shed again, me and Rory. We had just finished a chess game that ended in stalemate and neither of us felt like a rematch. Rory just wanted to hear about Conor's house.

'There was a pond in the garden as well, with a net over it.'

'That's so a heron doesn't come flying in and grab the goldfish,' he said.

'But that's a fish!'

'That's what I said. Goldfish.'

'No, the heron.'

'What are you talking about?'

'A heron's a fish.'

'You're thinking of a herring, Kev. Jesus!'

'Hey, wouldn't that be funny – a big fish flying in and nabbing the goldfish.'

Rory laughed like he could see it. 'Hey, that reminds me about what Sully said about goldfish,' he said.

'What?'

'He said that goldfish are small because they're kept in small goldfish bowls. Like if you put them into bigger bowls, then they'd grow bigger.'

'Yeah?'

'Yeah.'

'That's mad,' I said. 'So whales could be goldfish that broke out of their bowls and escaped to sea.'

'Yeah,' Rory said, laughing.

'And your da would be smaller if he had stayed driving his little taxi.'

Rory frowned like he had to think about that one.

'What about your Uncle Davy then?' he said.

'What about him?'

'That prison he was in must have been like a real goldfish bowl, like him stuck circling around in the one place and guards watching his every move.'

'I think it's more like an aquarium, Rory. You know, trying to stay clear of the bigger fish and hoping none of them would eat you.'

'I don't think you'd last long in prison, Kev,' Rory said and laughed.

'That's not funny, Rory. And another thing – you make sure not to blab that to anyone about Davy being inside.'

'Kevin, I knew about your uncle being inside ages ago. My da told me. And anyway it's all well forgotten cos it happened so long ago and in a different country.'

I went back to placing the chess pieces in the lunch box

and thought about the size of Conor's house and wondered why Conor wasn't a giant.

'You should've seen his kitchen, Rory. The size of the fridge!'

'Bigger than my fridge?' Rory said.

'Yeah. So big you could hide Lunchbox in it.'

'What about my da?'

'Hey, it wasn't *that* big.'

Rory laughed.

But I didn't feel like laughing.

'What?' Rory said.

'Nothing.'

'Did something happen?'

'No! Nothing happened. It was just ...'

'What?'

'Just when he started talking about his da and the garden and Old Trafford it was like ... I dunno, like he went off somewhere really sad.'

'Did he say anything about getting the football gear back? Did he mention that at all, like how it just turned up? That must have cheered him up.'

I snapped the plastic and pressed down each side to make sure the lid wouldn't come off.

'Kevin.'

'What?'

'You didn't give it back, did you?'

'I told you I did, didn't I?'

'Yeah, but you didn't, did you? I know you didn't.'

I looked at Rory and he just kept staring at me.

'Look, Rory, I tried to give it back after the game. I left it all in the car but his ma found it before I could get clear and she called me and handed it to me. And then I had to pretend it was my gear and I told her that Conor could have it cos his was gone, but she nearly started crying at that so I had to scarper.'

'With the bag?'

'Yeah, with the bloody bag. And if I'd brought it with me today then I'd have had to explain how I got it. And then his mother might have called the guards and they'd want to know how we saved stuff before the car got torched. And then they'd want to know about all the other stuff in the car and what we'd done with that.'

'You said your Uncle Davy brought that back.'

'He dropped it at the front of the house.'

'Are you sure? Like, did she mention anything about that when she was talking about the car?'

'Hey, how could I ask her anything? And she didn't say anything.'

'But you're sure he gave it back?'

'Rory, I saw him with my own two eyes outside the house. Now can you drop it?'

'OK, but you have to return the gear.'

'I know I've to return it. I'm going there tomorrow. His ma's going back to work and he'll be at his granda's for the day so that means we can go over and just leave it at the side of the house.'

'We?'

'Yeah. Me and you! You can say you're coming over to my house. I'll tell Ma I'm coming over here to you. We can cycle. I'll give you a backer.'

Rory went silent like he was trying to think of a way of getting out of it.

'Remember, Rory, you took stuff as well. You took stuff that was worth even more than the stuff I took.'

'Yeah. But it got taken back, didn't it?'

'Yeah. But you didn't have to do it, did you? Davy did it for you. And now you're leaving me to do the dirty work on my own. It's not fair, Rory.'

'OK,' Rory said, 'OK, but I'm in charge of the bike.'

13

I left Rory minding the bike and I strolled across the road and into the driveway of Conor's house. I went up to the door to knock on it and then stopped, cos I had the kitbag in my hand, and the ball, and how was I going to explain all that if someone came out. I turned and went round the corner of the house and placed everything on the ground and then went back to the door. I lifted the metal knocker and tapped it on the door three times. Then I waited. I looked back out at the road and I could see Rory standing up now like he was wondering what I was doing. I couldn't shout out to him that I was just making sure there was nobody in the house. I waited a few more seconds and when I turned to look out towards the road Rory was making these movements with his hands like he was directing traffic or something.

'What?' I said when I raced back across the road to him. 'Is there someone coming?'

'No, you eejit, Kevin. I wasn't calling you out here. I was just telling you to get on with it. That's all.'

'Jesus, Rory. You'd want to be more careful with your hands then. Just as well you weren't in an auction room or you'd owe a few million to someone.'

'Will you shut up talking, Kevin, and just get it over with? I want to go home.'

I ran back towards Conor's door, but this time, instead of knocking, I just walked quickly down the side of his house, grabbed the gear and went round the back. Everything was the same as the day before except there was a football on the grass near the soccer goal. I walked over to the deck and took the football out of the shopping bag and threw it over beside the other one. I put the kitbag on the decking and was about to turn away when I thought of a brilliant idea. I picked up the bag and went down the garden to the clothes line. I was going to hang all the gear on it when I thought of an even better idea still. I took up the bag and ran to the first of the trees.

I took out the jersey and hung it from a branch with the arms dangling. I did the same with the shorts and the socks and then stood back. It looked deadly, like they'd all fallen from the sky. I looked around to see what I'd do with the football boots. I'd cleaned them after the game so they were as good as when I'd found them. The pond! I went over to it and leaned over it and placed each boot like they'd also fallen from the sky and been saved by the net. I looked around then to see where to put the kitbag. I decided the best place for it was on top of the goalie net.

My phone rang. It was Rory.

'What?'

'There's a boy coming up the road on a bike and he looks like it might be Conor. He looks like you – small and with the same hair. Yeah, it's him. He's turning into the house. You'd better hide.'

I cut Rory off and raced down the path between the trees until I came to the shed. I went round the back of it and then peeped out to look towards the house. Conor appeared, wheeling his bike, and made straight for his football. He'd forgotten the ball and now he was back to get it. But when he saw the second ball he kinda shook his head like he was seeing things. He went slowly over to it and lifted it up. I could see him holding it close to his chest and rolling it in his hands, examining it. Then he looked up and saw the kitbag on the goal.

He dropped the ball at his feet and reached up slowly and took the bag down. He opened it quickly like he was expecting to find stuff in it. He scratched his forehead and looked about him, trying to figure what the hell was going on.

Then he saw his football gear on the branches. He made a sprint for the tree and pulled off the jersey first and turned it round to read his name on the back. He held it up high to admire it, then let it fall over his face and I could hear him laughing out loud. He lowered the jersey and lifted his head to peer up at the sky. His head made a circle as he searched for some sign or other. Then, not finding any, he placed the jersey over his arm as he picked off the shorts and the socks. He gathered them together with the jersey and held them close to his chest like Mandy Quirke holding her baby. Then he saw the boots and he froze for a second or two before lifting his gaze once more to the sky. Then he ran to the pond and leaned over it and for a second I thought he was going to fall in, but he didn't. He pulled out the boots and turned them in his hands and looked back up into the sky once more. He stared at all the stuff he'd collected and I could see his hand go to his eyes like he was wiping them. Then he stuffed all the gear into the bag and zipped it shut. As he made his way back to the bike, he was glancing up at the sky in case something else might fall.

He had the bag on his shoulder and his precious Man U football on the carrier and seemed all set to leave, but then he changed his mind cos he got off the bike and took the bag off. He went over to the back door and tried to open it but it was locked. He went over to the little bar and went in behind the counter and I couldn't see him behind the curtain. I came out from behind the shed and moved down a couple of trees to try and see what he was doing.

He reappeared almost immediately carrying a tin can. He took a key out of the can and went back to the door and slid it open. Then he disappeared inside with the kitbag. I waited for a minute or two and he came out again without the bag, slid the door shut and locked it. He put the key back in the can and disappeared behind the curtain once more. Then he was back in view again. He turned to look up the garden and raised his face up to the sky and I could see his big beamer of a smile even from where I was watching. He took up the bike with the Man U ball on the carrier and disappeared down the side of the house. I waited until my phone rang before I made a move.

'He's gone,' Rory said when I answered the call.

I told Rory what I'd done with the football gear and the boots and he thought it was the funniest thing ever.

'His ma is going to be really puzzled as well,' I said.

'Yeah. How is she going to explain that?'

'I shouldn't have bothered bringing the ball back, though,' I said.

'Why not?' Rory asked.

'Because now he has two balls.'

Rory laughed.

'Everyone has two balls, Kev. Like, is there something you're not telling me?'

14

We were back in the field and both of us feeling good cos Conor had gotten his precious gear back. I could try and forget about him now, especially since he believed his da was keeping an eye on him.

I had bought two cans of Coke and I gave one to Rory. We sat on the side of Rory's frying pan of a pitch and Rory was texting on his phone while I stared up at the clouds, trying to see shapes of things in them.

But even though I could try now to forget about Conor and his dead da and Jenny, I couldn't forget about the gun up in Adam's room. The trip to the carnival and to Conor's house had moved it to the back of my mind. But now it was really bothering me. I didn't know who I could say it to. Rory would be too frightened if I told him, and he'd have to tell his da, and then the guards would be down at our door and Adam would be hauled away. And Ma would be upset and could even get into trouble, and Uncle Davy might too, since he had a prison record. Davy was probably the best one to say it to, but the only problem was that it was hard to get time to talk to him without Adam being there with him.

'Adam and Davy get on like a house on fire,' I said when Rory put his phone away.

'More like a car on fire if you ask me,' he said.

The two of us laughed even though it was nothing to laugh about.

Then we were quiet and I looked off up into the hills and thought about Cokey Mulligan. Maybe somebody would need to take Adam up into those hills and beat the crap out of him. Rory's da said it was the only way some of the kids on the estate could ever hope to learn. Rory took a sip from his Coke and gargled it before swallowing.

'Do you like your da?' I asked him.

'Jesus! What kind of a stupid question is that? Everyone likes their da.'

'Do you think my Uncle Davy would make a good da?'
'Davy?'

'Yeah. Do you like him?'

'What's that got to do with anything?'

'I'm just asking you, Rory. Do you like Uncle Davy? I like your da even though he's a bit of a nark sometimes.'

'Hey!'

'You know what I mean, Rory. Like the way he watches everything you do. Like if you didn't wipe your arse properly, he'd know about it.'

'Yeah well, I don't really know your Uncle Davy, do I?' Rory said. 'Except sometimes he has a kinda scary look in his eye.'

'That's not true, Rory,' I said.

But it was true what Rory said. The look he gave Adam that time in the sitting room was really scary. And that time he binned the chess pieces and shouted at me and Ma. That was scary too.

'Da says he's one of those guys who wants to make a lot of money quickly without having to work too hard for it,' Rory said.

I thought about Uncle Davy in prison and what that must have been like for him. It made me think of striped goldfish packed into a tiny goldfish bowl and then I remembered once seeing a goldfish with a piece of its tail missing that some other fish had bitten off.

'It's kinda sad though.'

'What is?'

'I dunno ... just Ma ...'

'What?'

'I dunno. Just the way she's kinda changed towards him all of a sudden, like she's avoiding him, like something has changed for her around him. Maybe it's since ...'

'What?'

'I thought they might get on ... and he might have been able to ... you know ... especially at the start when it seemed like he might help her with Adam. But now it feels like ... like he just wants to take Adam away from her. It doesn't feel good any more. It's like Ma doesn't like Uncle Davy much at all now. I never see her laughing the way she does when she's with ... oh my God!'

'What? What? What's going on?'

I didn't want to answer Rory, and I didn't have to, cos someone shouted his name and when we looked behind us, we could see Mags Boylan coming towards us wheeling her ma's pink bike and followed by her little brother, Jake, who was carrying a skateboard that was way too big for him.

Rory stood up and brushed loose bits of grass off his shorts.

'Hey, Mags!' he called out to her like he was mad excited to see her. I said nothing. Rory put his hand out towards Jake and they high-fived each other.

'Hiya, Rory,' Jake said in a tiny shy voice. He glanced at me and then looked away towards Mags, who was looking at Rory.

I felt like asking her what she wanted but I kept my mouth shut in case it came out bad.

'Jake has me demented, Rory. He says you promised him you'd teach him how to use the skateboard.'

'He can hardly carry it,' I said. 'How's he going to go on it? He's too young.'

'I'm not too young,' Jake said like he might start crying any second. 'I'm seven.' He looked at Mags and then at Rory.

Mags didn't even look at me, just acted like I wasn't there.

'Hey, don't worry about it, Jakey,' Rory said. 'I saw you on it already, didn't I? I'll have you doing jumps and kickflips before you're eight.'

'I'm eight next week,' Jake said and Mags and Rory laughed.

I didn't see the big deal with skateboards but Rory had one and liked messing about with it on his own road.

'I'll call down to your house in a little while, Mags. Me and Kevin are finished here anyway.' He looked at me and I shrugged like I didn't care what he did.

It was then we heard the noise of a speeding car somewhere in the distance and then the squeal of brakes. Mags grabbed Jake by the hand and pulled him towards her.

'We've to go, Jake. And you should come with us too, Rory.' But Rory was watching the far end of the pitch like I was, and we both saw the car nosing into view. Mags quickly turned her bike and pushed it back towards the path and snapped at Jake cos he was paying too much attention to the car that was now down at the end of the pitch. I saw Mags stare at it in horror and then she got up on the bike and pedalled away, with Jake running after her and shouting for her to wait. Rory shaded his eyes with his hand.

'That's ...'

'Adam,' I said.

'I know it's Adam. But look at the car.'

'Ah, no!' I shouted.

Adam didn't look in a hurry this time as he cruised the Civic towards us and stopped before he got as far as the goalposts.

Me and Rory watched him. He left the engine running and got out, and Madser got out the other side. There was no sign of Lunchbox.

'Well hello there, boys,' Adam said, and Madser sniggered as he leaned over the passenger door.

'What do yiz think of me new set of wheels?'

'That's Sully's car,' Rory shouted.

'You'd better not wreck it, Adam,' I warned him.

'Well, Short Arse, me and Madser are going to test-drive this piece of crap and see what kind of speed we can get out of it. Then we'll maybe ... hey ... have a little bonfire.'

'You can't do that,' Rory shouted. 'You can't.'

'Sully is a friend of Ma's, so I wouldn't burn it if I was you,' I said.

'Yeah, well maybe he won't be a friend after today.'

Rory pulled his phone from his pocket and held it up in front of his face.

'I'm going to ring my da and he'll ring the guards so you'd better not do anything to that car.'

Adam slammed the door shut and came charging at Rory. He grabbed his hand and twisted it. The phone dropped to the ground and Adam picked it up and peered at the screen.

'Nice phone. I always wanted one of these.'

'I'm telling Davy!' I shouted. 'If you torch Sully's car, I'm telling Davy.'

Adam grabbed Rory by the wrist once more and I could see Rory wince with the pain.

'I'm taking this car, and me and Madser are gonna have a bit of fun with it. See? And then I'm gonna torch it. Is that OK with you, Rory?'

He twisted Rory's wrist until Rory nodded.

'Hey, Madser, Rory says it's OK.'

Madser laughed and sat into the passenger seat. But Adam wasn't finished with Rory yet. 'And as for the phone,' he said, his big claw of a hand still clamped around Rory's bony wrist. 'You can tell your auld fella that you lost it. And if I hear that you've said anything different to him, then I'll call around and it's his fat taxi that I'll be driving next. Do ya hear me?'

'Yeah!' Rory cried.

Adam pushed him away. Then he looked at me. 'And you can tell Davy if you want to, you little rat. But I don't think he'll mind too much.'

He turned away and got into the driver's seat and banged the door shut. He drove off slowly till he came to the slope and then he gunned the engine and the car bounced over it and disappeared off down towards the main road.

'Are you all right?' I asked Rory.

Rory didn't look at me but kept his head down and held his sore wrist with his other hand.

'Just leave me alone, Kevin, OK? Just leave me alone.'

He ran off towards the estate and I hoped he'd have enough sense not to tell his da or anyone else what had happened.

I watched him run all the way, wondering if he'd go home or if he'd go around to Mags Boylan's house. He headed for home and never looked back even once to see where I was. I took up my football and ran down to the other end of the pitch and stood on top of the slope and peered across the other playing pitches to the road and the shops beyond them. There was no sign of the car. I thought of Sully and how upset he was going to be and then I looked up at the hills and thought that it mightn't be a bad idea at all if someone took Adam up there to teach him a lesson.

15

As soon as I was in the door I called out for Ma, but the house stayed silent. I flew up the stairs and into Adam's room. I headed straight for his hidey-hole and pulled back the carpet. If the money was still there, I was going to take it all and give it to Sully to fix his car, and I didn't care what Adam might do about it.

But before I could lift out the board, I heard the front door opening. I snapped the carpet back in place and went quickly out of the room and stood at the top of the stairs to listen. It was Davy, and he'd gone straight into the kitchen cos I could hear the water splashing into the kettle.

I banged down the stairs and stood in the kitchen doorway.

'Where's the fire?' Davy asked.

'Davy! Listen. You have to do something.'

He put the kettle down.

'What's going on?'

'It's Adam!' I gasped. 'It's stupid Adam.'

The front door opened and when I turned around I could see it was Ma on her way in, carrying a shopping bag.

'What happened?' Davy asked as Ma came past me into the kitchen.

'It's Adam. It's always Adam.'

'What's happened to Adam? Has there been an accident?' Ma asked, her voice all concern, like she was thinking he'd been knocked down by a car or something. If only!

'Ma, he stole Sully's car.'

'Adam?!' Ma cried, shocked. She dropped the shopping bag with a clunk on the kitchen table.

'Yeah. He was in the field with it and he twisted Rory's arm and stole his phone.' I turned to Davy. 'Davy, you have to talk to him. He's going to burn the car.'

Ma turned to Davy and stared at him like it was his job to handle it.

'What? This hasn't anything to do with me,' Davy said, and started filling the kettle once more.

'For Christ's sakes! He's after taking Mr Sullivan's car. You can't let him get away with that.'

'Ring him, Davy! Ring him and tell him he can't do it.'

'I'm not ringing Adam. Anyway, how do you know it was Adam who took it?'

'Because I was there. Madser was with him. He said he was going to burn it.' I looked at Ma. 'One of you has to ring him.'

Ma stared at Davy.

'You need to do something about this. You can't let him destroy Sully's car.'

'Oh, it's "Sully" now, is it?'

'I'm going upstairs,' Ma said.

'But Ma, Sully is our friend.'

I grabbed her by her jacket before she could leave the kitchen.

'Your Uncle Davy needs to ring him. You know he won't listen to me.'

I looked towards Davy but he was acting like we weren't even there. He switched on the kettle and took a mug down from the press. Ma sighed like she was really tired and I let go of her jacket.

'I'll ring him from upstairs, Kevin,' she said. 'But you know it won't do any good.'

She turned round and left the kitchen. I was going to follow her but Davy called me.

'He won't burn it,' he said, slopping old teabags out of the teapot into the sink.

'He will burn it. That's what he always does.'

'Well, he won't burn it this time.'

'How do you know?'

'Because I just know.'

'You don't know him the way I do. He's evil, Davy. Adam is evil.'

Davy laughed. He just stared at the kettle and laughed.

'It's not funny, Davy.'

'I know it's not funny. He's not the sharpest knife in the drawer, but he's not evil. He's too stupid to be evil.'

'But Davy –'

'Listen to me, Kevin. If Adam did take the car, then I'll give him a bollocking when he comes in. But if he did take it ... well, then I think I know the reason why he did.'

'Why?'

'Because he's pissed off with yer man, Sully – whatever you call him.'

'What?'

'Well, for starters, Sullivan accused him of breaking into the community centre, even though your ma says he was here at the time.'

'But Davy, he wasn't here. I know he wasn't here.'

'Well, I'm telling you he was. OK?'

Davy's eyes were wide and staring right at me. I looked away from him down to the floor. 'And then, to make matters worse, your ma goes and gets herself a job down there. How do you think Adam felt when he heard that? They're accusing him of breaking and entering and his own ma goes and stabs him in the back.'

'She didn't stab him in the back. She lied for him.'

Davy pointed his finger at me. 'Listen to me, you! I don't particularly care if Adam took that creep's car. OK? It doesn't bother me in the slightest. And do you know why? He's a bloody smarmy bastard who goes around pretending to do good when he's really up to something else.'

'I don't know what you're talking about. Sully isn't smarmy – and he's not a creep either.'

'Do you even know what the word "sully" means? Do you?'

'That's his name!'

'Yeah it's his name, but do you know what it means when you use the word "sully"? It means dirty. Yeah. That's what it means and that's probably why people call him that because they know what he's up to behind my back and everyone else's back.'

I couldn't believe Davy was talking about Sully like that. He put two new teabags into the teapot and poured in boiling water from the kettle.

'You stay away from him from now on. Do you hear me? I won't have any nephew of mine involved with the likes of him.' He stirred the teabags with a spoon and I turned to leave.

When I came out into the hallway, I saw Ma halfway down the stairs with her phone in her hand.

'I couldn't get him on his phone,' she said. 'But Sully's car is after pulling up outside.

Davy came out from the kitchen and went into the sitting room to look out through the front window. I went in to stand beside him as Ma opened the front door.

Sully was getting out of his car and I could see him look towards Ma. Then he caught sight of Davy in the window and he seemed to hesitate like he wasn't sure now why he'd called.

'What did I tell you?' Davy said. 'Adam never did anything to that fool's car.'

I left Davy's side and went out the door to stand beside Ma on the front step. Sully stood outside the gate and his face was red and his bottom lip pulled in like he was chewing it.

'It was Adam, Rose. I know it was him. He took the car and drove it through the fields and slashed the seats and spilled Coke all over them.'

Ma moved off the step and went out to have a look for herself. I followed along behind. Sully moved around to the front of the car and waved a hand at the side that was filthy with dirt and that had its wing mirror dangling from a piece of wire.

'I can clean the dirt off. That's not the problem. It's the inside. Look at the state of the inside.'

Sully opened the back door of the car and Ma stooped down to have a look.

'It's the same in the front seat. And, as well as that, I think there might be a problem with the suspension.'

Ma stood there with her arms folded like she didn't know what to say.

'Your insurance will pay for it.'

We all looked behind us back to the door. Davy was standing in the doorway holding a mug of tea in one hand and a cigarette in the other. 'That's what insurance is for, isn't it?' he said. Then he turned and went back indoors.

Sully looked from the door to Ma. His face was getting redder and his hair was lathered in sweat and sticking to his forehead. His jacket looked like it was stained from sitting in the driver's seat. He was squeezing his lips together like he was trying to keep in his anger, and his hands were made into fists down by his sides.

'What do you want me to do?' Ma said.

'What do I want you to do?' Sully said, panting like he was breathless. 'Get the little bastard to pay for it.'

'Don't call him a bastard. Please.'

'What do you want me to call him? And what do you want me to do about it? Lie down and just take it? Is that it? Is that what I've to do? Is that what everyone in this bloody place has to do just so that your precious Adam can keep doing what he does?'

He got into the front seat of the car, which had a black plastic bag on it, and slammed the door shut. Then he got back out again and ripped off the side mirror and threw it into the passenger seat. He started the engine and moved away, the car rattling a little like there was a marble loose somewhere in the engine. Ma stood watching till he turned the corner and was gone from sight. She saw me eyeing her.

'Don't look at me like that, Kevin. Don't you dare look at me like that.'

Later that evening when Adam came in, Ma didn't say anything to him. She just left the kitchen as soon as he appeared and didn't speak to him or anyone else. After a little while she put on her coat and went out the front door. She didn't say where she was going and I don't know if Davy and Adam even noticed. They were in the sitting room talking. I crept halfway down the stairs and listened to what they were talking about.

'So what have we on tonight?' Adam asked.

'We're staying in.'

'We're not going out?'

'We're staying in, and I'm staying with you cos it's the only way I can be sure you won't run out and do something else as stupid as you did earlier.'

'I was never going to burn it, Davy. I just wanted to put the frighteners on him, like you said.'

'And what about this phone that you took from Baldy's son. Whatever he's called – Rory. I don't want that causing trouble. Maybe you should give it to Kevin to give back to him.'

'I left it in the house.'

'What house?'

'The empty house on the cul-de-sac. I left it there somewhere. Do you want me to go and get it?'

'No, leave it. I don't want you stirring out of here until I tell you to. We've got too much to lose.'

'All right, Davy. Anyway, the little prick isn't going to tell Baldy cos I told him what'll happen if he does.'

'Are you sure about that?'

'Yeah.'

Then they were quiet and I could hear a beer can snapping open.

'And take it easy with that stuff too.'

A second can hissed.

'Did you get those toys for the house like I asked?'

'Yeah, I got plenty.'

Toys for the house? I didn't have a clue what that was about.

The telly suddenly came to life with the sound of a football match.

'Davy?'

'What?'

'How long will you stay there?'

'Where?'

'Up north.'

'I don't know.'

'Is it for good?'

'I don't know. Now shut up, will ya. I want to watch this game.'

I crept back up to my room and lay on the bed to think before I turned on the telly. Why was Davy going up north? Maybe he had the offer of a job in a garage up there and maybe he was going there cos he'd given up on Ma. And why had Adam to get toys? What was that about? Unless it was for someone's kids that Davy knew who maybe lived north of the border and they were going to visit. Or maybe it could be they were getting stuff together to sell for the Christmas market. And maybe the gun in Adam's room was also a toy? But it didn't look like a toy. It felt heavy and looked real. My brain felt sore from trying to figure it out so I thought of other things instead.

I wondered what Conor was doing and if he was still staring up at the sky with a puzzled look on his face. He had the same look when I handed him his phone that day in the carnival. I thought of Rory and how upset he'd been at losing his phone. And then I thought that maybe if I got Rory's phone back, then me and Rory could be mates again.

16

The deserted house looked gloomy and the back garden was full of shadows that I didn't want to stare too long at. As soon as I pushed the door in, I could get the smell of pee, cigarettes and damp. I stood in the open doorway and glanced around the kitchen, hoping Rory's phone might be somewhere in clear view. The place was in a worse mess than the last time I'd been there.

The sink was full of empty pizza boxes and the plastic table had empty cans of Coke and beer on it like skittles knocked over. The floor was cluttered with plastic bottles, cigarette boxes and crisp bags. The wheelchair was still there, as well as the old armchair.

I searched among the cans on the table but there was no sign of the phone. The worktop was covered in bits of stale pizza crust and manky-looking slices of rubbery cheese, and something that looked like fruit that had blue hairy mould growing out of it. It was gross. I picked up a kitchen knife with a rusty blade and poked my way along the counter with it but there was no sign of the phone there either. I scanned the floor and began moving pieces of rubbish with my foot.

Then I stepped into the hallway and I could see a black binbag sticking out from underneath the stairs. It had fallen over and had tipped some of its rubbish out onto the floor. It was pages and pages of stuff. There was something familiar about the bag and the type of pages that were in it. I picked some up and peered at them. It was the stuff from Conor's da's car. It was all the files that Rory found to do with the bank. I couldn't believe it. Davy hadn't brought it back. Then I thought maybe he didn't because it was all rubbish. Why would he bring back all the useless crap when it would just have to be thrown out anyway? Maybe he'd just brought back the cheque books.

I rooted down into the bag but found my hand touching something soft and squishy like old food so I pulled it out quickly and wiped my hand on bits of paper. Then a phone rang.

I stepped away from the stairs and stood in the doorway between the hall and the kitchen, and listened. The ringtone was the same as Rory's and was coming from the kitchen so I headed in there.

It was coming from the armchair. I pushed the wheelchair out of the way and poked down the side of the fat cushion, half-afraid I was going to meet something squishy again. But it was the phone I felt. I must have turned it off by accident because as soon as I pulled it clear of the chair, it stopped ringing. I held it up and looked at the screen. Mags Boylan's face smiled out at me.

I stuffed the phone into my pocket and was ready to head out the door when I heard noise from upstairs. It was like something dragging on floorboards. I could feel my heart pumping in my ears and all I wanted to do was run. The sound came again. There was someone up there. Suddenly I could hear fists pounding on a door and then a frightened voice.

'Hey! Let me out. Please! Let me out. Adam, please.'

It was Lunchbox. His squeaky pleading voice sounded exactly like it did when he was grabbing hold of the goal-post on the football pitch. For a second I didn't know what to do. I was going to scarper but instead I stood and listened to the pounding.

'Please, Adam! Please!'

I crept towards the bottom step and stared up. It sounded like he was trapped in the bathroom. I went halfway up the stairs and stopped. I took out my phone and turned on the little torchlight even though there was light enough coming in from the kitchen. The banging had stopped but I could hear Lunchbox's voice crying on the other side of the door.

'Lunchbox?' I called. 'Lunchbox, is that you?'

'Who's that?'

I took the final steps to the landing and looked towards the bathroom door. There was a bit of an old clothesline tied from the door handle to the banisters so the door couldn't be opened from the inside. And lying on the bare floorboards of the landing was Lunchbox's crutch. I moved the crutch out of the way with my foot and leaned my head in nearer the door.

'Lunchbox, it's me. Kevin.'

'Kevin. Is Adam down there?'

'There's only me here.'

'Get me out of here, Kevin, please.'

I grabbed at the piece of clothesline that was looped around the handle, untied it and yanked it off. Then I opened the door and shone the torch at Lunchbox's face. It was still wet from where he had been crying, and his cropped hair looked like it had been used as a duster. His chubby cheeks were red and marked with lines of dirt as if he had wiped them with filthy hands. And then the smell of the place hit my nose.

'This place is disgusting, Lunchbox.'

'What was I supposed to do? There's no water and the toilet's gone.'

I shone the torch around the room and could see where the toilet bowl and cistern had been, and the sink was gone too. There was nothing in the room except for a filthy-looking bath that Lunchbox had crapped in.

'What are you doing here, Lunchbox?'

'Adam and Madser locked me in.' He wiped his face with his hand but only smeared more dirt onto the mess. 'We were playing cards and whoever lost was supposed to spend a night here on their own.'

'And let me guess. You lost.'

'Yeah, but I said I didn't want to stay here on my own. So Adam and Madser dragged me up here, took my phone off me and locked me in.'

'Why do you hang around with them, Lunchbox? They treat you like a piece of crap.'

I stood aside and let him move past me out the door. We went down the stairs. When we got as far as the kitchen and daylight, he stopped and looked at me.

'What are you doing here anyway?'

'I came looking for Rory's phone. Adam took it when he stole Sully's car.'

'Yeah, Sully's car. They were talking about that when they left me here.'

'Adam has a gun, Lunchbox. Should I tell Uncle Davy?'

Lunchbox laughed.

'What's funny about that? He has a gun, Lunchbox. A real gun! He has it hidden in his room.'

'You saw it?'

'Yeah, he has it wrapped in clingfilm.'

'That's not Adam's gun.'

'How do you know it's not his gun?'

'Adam doesn't like guns.'

'How do you know he doesn't like guns?'

'Guns freak him out.'

'You're crazy, Lunchbox. Nothing freaks Adam out.'

'Adam doesn't want anything to do with guns. He says if you carry a gun, you'll only end up using it.'

'Adam said that?'

'Yeah.'

'But what about knives then?'

'He never carries a knife either.'

'Well, who cut up Sully's car then, and all the sofas in the community centre? And the chess sets?'

'That was Madser. It's him that's big into knives. Adam just took the cans of Coke and wrote the graffiti, but it was Madser who went off on a mad one slashing everything.'

'Well, Adam has a gun in his room. I saw it.'

'Then he's minding it for someone.'

'Who?'

'Probably your Uncle Davy.'

'Davy?'

'Yeah, your Uncle Davy.'

'What does Davy want a gun for? Like he's just come ... I mean ... like ... that's just crazy, Lunchbox.'

Lunchbox pulled up his dirty grey tracksuit bottoms and tightened the string on them. Then he pulled his hood up over his head and shivered.

'OK. It's not your uncle's gun then. But listen, I'm freezing my arse off so no more questions.'

'Just tell me why would my uncle need a gun? Is someone after him?'

Lunchbox sniggered at that.

'Kevin, do you know who your Uncle Davy is?'

'What? What are you talking about?'

'Your Uncle Davy, Kevin. Your Uncle Davy is afraid of nobody. Everybody is scared of him.'

'So why does he need a gun, then?'

'He's probably planning a job.'

'What kind of job? What job are you talking about, Lunchbox?'

'Look, I don't know what job he's planning but I know he needs money.'

'He has loads of money, Lunchbox. He's always flashing the cash.'

'Yeah! He likes to flash it but he's up to his eyes in debt with your man Deegan he works for. Adam told me that. And he told me Deegan's garage is just a front for laundering money and Davy wants out of there before the roof falls in on top of him.'

'You think he's going to rob Deegan then and do a runner?'

'I don't know, Kevin. It could be he has to do a bit of dirty work for Deegan to clear his debt. I don't know what he's planning, Kevin, but he's planning something, especially if he's got Adam minding a gun for him. Remember, he's a jailbird, Kevin. You do know that, don't you?'

'Of course I know that. But why would he risk ending up there again?'

Lunchbox suddenly took hold of the side of the wheelchair. 'See this wheelchair, Kevin. Who do you think that belongs to?'

'I dunno.'

'Cokey Mulligan, that's who.'

'What? That's crazy.'

'And who put him in that wheelchair?'

'I don't know. Who?'

'Your Uncle Davy, that's who!'

'Davy did that to Cokey Mulligan?'

'You haven't a clue, Kevin, do ya, about what's really going on in this estate?'

I stared at the wheelchair, then up at Lunchbox's dirty face.

'Davy?'

'Yeah. Cokey Mulligan was moving in on Adam's patch of the estate where he sells most of his stuff. Your uncle warned Cokey Mulligan off but he didn't heed the warning.'

'Who told you all this?'

'Adam told us all about it. He's always talking about his Uncle Davy.'

'It was Davy brought Cokey Mulligan up the mountain?'

'Yeah, him and some guys he brought out from town. They beat him so badly he needed crutches to get around and sometimes a wheelchair. And then a few days ago Adam and Madser met him somewhere out on the road. Cokey was heading to the shops on his own in the wheelchair and carrying the crutches on his lap. Adam and Madser just tossed him out of the chair and took it, along with the crutches, thinking it was funny. They gave me one of the crutches and I thought they were being kind because of my sore leg. But they were just having the laugh and maybe hoping that Cokey Mulligan would hear that I was hobbling around on one of his crutches and taking the piss.'

Lunchbox moved to the back door.

'What's Davy going to do, Lunchbox?'

'I don't know. All I know is it's going to be very hard for Adam to refuse him anything he asks. Like, I'm sure you've noticed how he's always trying to impress him. He hero-worships him. Haven't you noticed how he dresses like him. He even walks and talks like him too. If it wasn't so scary it'd be funny. But then again he mightn't be up to anything.'

'What do you mean?'

'Look, Kevin. I don't know. Your Adam can be weird. Like the other day I heard him tell Madser he was going to make a shitload of money from doing a bit of babysitting.'

'Babysitting. Adam? Babysitting?'

Lunchbox laughed.

'See what I mean. Weird.'

Lunchbox opened the back door and stepped down carefully onto the garden path. I watched him walk away slowly before he stopped and put one hand against the wall of the house.

'Will I get you the crutch?' I said.

'No way. Cokey Mulligan won't always be in a wheel-chair, you know.'

17

I ran all the way to Rory's house, thinking about everything that Lunchbox had said. He had to be wrong about it though. There was no way the gun belonged to Davy. There was no way Davy was going to risk going back to prison just when he was getting used to life outside. And as for Cokey Mulligan, whoever beat him up did the whole estate a favour – even Ma said so. Everyone said he had it coming to him, so if Davy did beat him up, then maybe that was OK.

I sprinted onto Rory's road and hopped the wall again because the gate was locked, with the taxi in behind it. Mags Boylan's pink bike was there leaning against the fence at the side.

I eyed it as I rang the bell. Some day someone was going to steal it on her cos she never seemed to bother locking it just cos it was her ma's. I rang the bell again but still there was no answer. I waited and then pressed the bell a third time. This time the door opened and Rory was there.

'Da's asleep, Kevin. So don't keep pressing the bell.'

'Here,' I said and handed him his phone.

He looked down at it and his eyes widened and his mouth fell open. He took the phone and peered at the screen.

'How did you get it back?'

'I stole it back. OK?'

'Thanks.'

'It just needs to be recharged. It's working cos I heard it ring.'

'That was my ma ringing to see if anyone had found it.'

'You told her you lost it?'

'Yeah.'

'You didn't say anything then about what happened to your wrist – and Sully's car?'

'What do you think?'

'Good. Anyway, he got it back. Sully got it back, his car, and you got back your phone.'

Rory came out onto the step and pulled the door a little behind him.

I nodded towards Mags Boylan's bike. 'I see you have a visitor.'

Rory's face went bright red. 'Feck's sake,' he said, 'I've to go down and get my school gear when Ma comes in from work and Mags wants to come with me.'

Then we heard the sound of dance music coming from his sitting room and Rory groaned. The music got louder.

'Jesus! I'd better go back in, Kevin, or she'll wake up Da, and he'll be down doing his angry bear impressions.'

When he turned to go back inside, I caught a glimpse of his wrist where Adam's nails had marked him.

'Hey!'

'What?'

'I'm sorry about what happened.'

He glanced at his wrist and shrugged like it was nothing to worry about. The music got louder again.

'For God's sake!' he wailed and turned and disappeared inside, closing the door behind him.

I stood there for a moment like for some reason I didn't want to leave. I smiled, thinking about Rory and Mags Boylan out shopping for Rory's new uniform. She'd probably have a photo of Rory and herself together up on her Facebook page before the day was over.

I thought of Becky. Maybe I'd send her a photo of me in my green jumper and say something funny about it. Or maybe I wouldn't. Then I wondered: if Becky was on a chess board, what would she be? A rook! Yeah, she'd be the rook, cos she was a little bit chubby. But she was smart, so I could see her one day being the queen.

18

When I reached my road, I stopped and stared. There was a white Hiace van parked outside my house. It was parked in front of Davy's car and Davy had the bonnet of the van lifted and was leaning in over the engine. There was a small splat of bird crap on the top corner of the windscreen and on the white paint above it.

'Hiya, Davy,' I said and stood there to let him know that I was over my upset over Sully's car and the things he'd said about him. I knew it was Ma he was really annoyed with and I wondered if he'd spotted her with Sully that day at the carnival.

He turned his head and nodded at me.

'Hiya, bud,' he said, holding the long dipstick in his hand and inspecting it for the shine of oil.

'That's one bird who didn't think much of your van, Davy.'

Davy frowned, then looked where I was pointing and laughed. 'I'll get Adam to clean that.'

'Yeah, good luck with that.'

I went around to the footpath side so I could see clearly what he was doing. There was a plastic jug on the ground that Ma used for filling the iron with water.

'Do you need more water, Davy?'

'It's OK, Kev,' he said, sliding the dipstick back into place. 'She's full to the brim.'

He had one of Adam's old grey T-shirts on him and it had fingers of oil smeared across the belly.

'Who owns the van? Is it from the garage?'

Davy didn't seem to hear me. He was busy cleaning the rim of the oil lid before he put it back in place.

'Are you getting a new job or something, Davy?'

'A job?' He straightened his body and held the oily rag in his fingers as he rubbed his forehead with the back of his hand. 'A job? Sure, I have a job, Kevin.'

'What's the van for, then? You look like you're getting it ready to go somewhere.'

Davy frowned and peered straight at me.

'What's up with you, bud? What's with all the questions?'

'Nothing,' I said. He turned away and screwed the oil lid into place then banged it shut with the flat of his hand. I couldn't think of anything else to ask him so I went inside to see if I could sneak into Adam's room and check for sure what kind of gun it was.

But Adam was still in there playing a game so loud it sounded like there was a war going on. I checked the fridge for food but there was nothing there I could eat so I headed for the community centre.

As soon as I opened the door, I got the whiff of fresh paint and I could see Sully had replaced the two black leather sofas with two new ones, and the place had been cleaned so you'd never think that Adam had been in there.

Ma was behind the counter when I came into the café. I ordered a chicken salad sandwich off her and a Coke and went to sit at a table on my own. Mandy Quirke and two of her friends were sitting two tables down from me. Her new baby was fast asleep in a buggy with its mouth open and a soother lying on its chest. The three of them were talking about the baby, about who she was like, and they were peering in at her and yapping so much I only hoped that they weren't going to waken her. The only other people in the café were two workmen in high-vis vests laying into a giant fry-up. They must have missed breakfast the way they were attacking the plate with their knives and forks.

Ma brought the sandwich and Coke over to me on a tray with a mug of coffee and her own toasted cheese sandwich on it as well.

She sat across from me and took a sip from her mug.

'Are you OK? You look a bit ... peaky.'

'Peaky?' I hadn't heard that one before.

'You look a bit pale, that's all.'

'I'm fine.'

She took a bite from her sandwich.

'I'll be a small bit late home this evening.'

I stared at her.

'Ma, you said this job wouldn't have too many hours.'

'And it doesn't. I have to go to a meeting after work. That's all.'

'Is Sully going to be there?'

Ma snatched at a wisp of hair that had escaped from the white cap they made her wear.

'I expect so. Like, he is the boss.'

'So what time will you be home at then?'

'Around five. But Davy said he's there all day today so ...'

'What?'

'He'll keep an eye on you.'

'I don't need anyone to keep an eye on me. Anyway, someone should keep an eye on Davy and Adam.'

Ma laughed. 'You're right there, Kev.'

The two of us took another bite from our sandwiches and then Ma had to put everything down while she tried to stick the piece of hair back underneath the cap.

'Do you have to wear that?'

'What's wrong with it?'

I smiled and slurped my Coke.

'You stop that awful noise or I'll have you thrown out.'

She turned to check the time on the wall clock.

'Ma?'

'What?'

'How long was Davy in prison in Manchester for?'

Ma looked around towards Mandy Quirke's table and then towards the counter.

'Keep your voice down, Kevin.'

'Ma, the whole estate knows he was inside.'

'I know, Kevin, but we don't have to advertise it.'

'Just tell me, Ma. How long?'

'Seven! He was sentenced to ten years but did about seven.'

'How come you never told me about him?'

'You were only four when it happened. It all went over your head.'

'You should have told me, Ma.'

'He didn't want you to know. He made me promise not to say anything.'

'Does Adam know?'

'Yeah! Don't look at me like that, Kevin. Adam was older than you. It was harder to keep it from him.'

'Did nobody go over to visit him?'

'I did early on – twice. Once with Adam but it was too upsetting for him so I never brought him again. And I went once on my own but he said he didn't want me over there leaving you all behind. But Rita visited him. She visited him regularly and brought things he liked and photos of the two of you.'

Ma took another sip of coffee and a bite from her sandwich and then she glanced around the café again.

'I don't know what to say to you, Kevin. I should have spoken more to you about him but ...'

'What?'

'It's just I thought maybe ... I don't know what I thought – I thought with him in the house more, he'd give you some time too – not just Adam.'

'Ma! He wanted to be in the house to be with *you*. It was nothing to do with Adam or me.' Before Ma could say anything to that, the door to the games room opened and Sully came through. Ma turned to see who I was looking at and she reddened when she saw who it was and she gave him a little secret wave. He smiled and nodded and then disappeared down a corridor to one of the meeting rooms.

'What? What are you looking at me like that for?'

'You're like a teenager, Ma.'

'I don't know what you're talking about, Kevin.'

'Sure, Ma.'

'He said he's going to start the club up again in a week or so.'

'Sully?'

'Yes, Kevin.'

'The chess as well?'

'Of course.'

I felt a little buzz of excitement, and Ma must have noticed cos she smiled at me. I looked away from her and examined the fresh paint on the wall to see if I could see where Adam had written his graffiti. There was no sign of it.

'Is he still angry over his car?'

'I told him I'll pay for any damage,' Ma said.

'I still have some money saved,' I said.

Ma smiled. 'Thanks, Kevin, you're a pet, but I still have a bit of savings myself, I'll have you know. Anyway he wants to talk to his insurance first before he decides what to do about fixing it.'

She drained her coffee and sighed. 'I need to have a smoke outside before I go back to work.'

I wiped away bits of mayonnaise off my lips with the back of my hand.

'Ma?'

'What?'

'What was Davy in prison for? Like, why did he get so long?'

Ma sighed again and peered at the outside door like she was really gasping for her fag.

'Did I not tell you that?'

'Ma! You told me nothing and I want to know.'

Mandy Quirke's table seemed to go suddenly quiet and I could see Ma glancing nervously over towards the three women.

'Look, Kevin, could this wait until this evening and we can talk about it at home.'

'I'd like to know about it now.'

The door down the corridor opened and Sully appeared, talking over his shoulder to a woman who was following him. Ma spotted them and got to her feet.

'I've to get back to work, Kevin.'

'Ma, it's only Sully.'

'He's my boss, Kevin.'

'But Ma –'

'I know, Kevin. I'll talk to you this evening. I promise. I'll be home straight after this meeting.'

19

Davy's car wasn't on the road when I got home. But the white van was there. Adam was still in his room. He had finished his war game and was now on his phone. He was talking to someone and saying how things were going to be different because he was going to get a regular job as a driver. I smiled when I heard that.

I went downstairs to see if Davy was in the house. He was out in the garden sitting in one of Ma's green plastic chairs with his two feet resting on another one opposite him. His hair looked wet, like he'd had a shower, and he was wearing a new blue T-shirt of his own and sunglasses like the fake Ray-Bans Adam sometimes sold. He nodded when he saw me standing in the doorway.

'Make me a fresh cup of tea there, Kevin, will ya?'

I turned round and went back into the kitchen and filled the kettle. I took my Man U mug from the press and put a tea bag in it. I watched Davy as the water boiled and started worrying again about the gun. I'd told Lunchbox it was a real one but maybe I was wrong to tell him that. Maybe it was just a pellet gun? What if I told Davy how I found it in Adam's room and asked him to examine it to see if it was real? What would he say? But what if Lunchbox was right and it was real – and belonged to Davy? Maybe he'd want to get rid of it if he realised I knew about it.

When I brought him out the mug of tea he took his feet down off the chair and placed the mug there instead. I waited for him to comment about the mug but he said nothing.

'Davy?'

He sipped the tea and made a face like it was too hot.

'What was ... what was England like?'

He put the mug back down and turned around to look up at me. I couldn't see his eyes, so I didn't know if he was annoyed or pleased that I asked him the question.

'I didn't see an awful lot of it, Kevin.'

I stood there waiting for him to say more but he went silent. I wanted him to tell me what it was like to be locked away for seven years but he looked away towards the fence at the end of the garden. And there was so much I wanted to ask him about Da. I wanted to find out what he remembered about him because I couldn't remember much at all. But then I felt bad because maybe I was just trying to remind him of stuff he wanted to forget. But the talk with Lunchbox was bugging me and the idea that Adam had a gun in his room was really scary.

'Adam shouldn't be drinking, Davy. It makes him turn nasty. Like the smoking is OK cos it just makes him dopey, but the drink makes him mean and he's going to do something bad and he'll end up in prison. He will. Will you talk to him, Davy? He'll listen to you.'

Davy sniffed and gave a little smile.

'He'll be all right, Kevin. He's just a bit wild, that's all. I was a bit like that myself at his age.'

'Where's your car? And who owns the white van?'

He took the mug in both hands and placed his feet back up on the chair.

'I left the car in the garage. I have the loan of the van for a few days.'

'Are you doing a job?'

He held the mug in one hand and lifted his sunglasses up above his eyes with the other, like he wanted to have a better look at me.

'I mean, could I go with you, if ... you know ... if you need help.'

'No, you're OK. I just have to give someone a hand to move a bit of furniture.'

'Is Adam going to help?' I asked.

'Yeah,' Davy said.

'Is that a good idea, Davy?'

He pushed the glasses back down with a finger and sipped his tea.

I watched him for a little bit and then I went back inside and up to my room. I lay on the bed and thought about what

I should do. I didn't know exactly what Lunchbox meant about Davy and Adam doing a job. The white van had me kinda confused cos it *was* the sort of van you could move furniture with. And if Davy was bringing toys with him up north, then that was a good sign he wasn't planning something that would get him into trouble. The more I thought about it, the more I made up my mind that it really was just a pellet gun, cos maybe they can look like the real thing, especially if they're wrapped in reams of clingfilm. I turned on the telly and watched *Friends*, and listened with one ear for Adam to leave his room and go downstairs to join Davy.

20

'Kevin.'

Ma shook my shoulder to waken me. For a second I didn't have a clue where I was or what time it was. She took the remote from my hand and turned off the telly. There was a bit of slobbery goo on the corner of my mouth and I wiped it off with my fingers.

'The telly is on downstairs and on in here, and every light left on in the house. Easy knowing who's paying the bills. Where's Davy and Adam?'

I rubbed the sleep from my eyes and sat up. 'They're not down there?'

'No.'

'They're moving furniture for a friend of Davy.'

'You're kidding me.'

'That's what Davy said.'

'Did they make you anything to eat?'

'No.'

I felt my stomach rumble at the mention of food.

'Well, then, I'll cook us some French toast and beans. Would you like that?'

I nodded and she smiled and went downstairs. I sat on the side of the bed trying to think. I could hear the rattle of the pan and press doors banging shut. I suddenly remembered what it was I had to do.

I went quietly as far as Adam's door and listened outside just in case he hadn't gone off to do his muscle work with Davy. I opened the door, pushed it slowly in and peered round the room. There was no sign of him, so I went quickly towards the hidey-hole and flipped back the carpet by the rad and lifted off the floorboard. I pulled out the ziplock bags, searching for the heavy one with the gun in it. But it wasn't there. The gun was gone. That meant Adam had taken it. But Lunchbox said Adam was afraid of guns. Then I remembered I'd already decided it was just a pellet gun. That was no big deal – if it *was* just a pellet gun.

I heard Ma's voice at the bottom of the stairs calling me down for the toast and beans. I waited until she was back in the kitchen before I left Adam's room and headed down to join her.

She sat across from me and gobbled her food like she hadn't eaten all day. She had her phone down beside her plate and she was smiling down at it like someone had sent her a funny text.

'Was Sully at your meeting?'

Ma looked up from the phone. 'Sorry, Kevin. What?'

'It doesn't matter, Ma.'

She picked up the phone and put it in her jeans pocket.

'Ma?'

'What?'

'You said you'd tell me.'

'Tell you what?'

'Ma. You know what. Davy.'

'Oh, Kevin, do we have to talk about that now? I'm just so tired. I'm going to take a shower and then I'm going to bed.'

'Ma, I want to know.'

'I told you, Kevin. I told you how long he was in for.'

'I want to know other stuff.'

I watched her eat and waited until she cleared her plate.

'Ma, you promised you'd tell me.'

'Oh, God! I don't know where to start.'

'Ma!'

'OK, Kevin. It's hard talking about it because it was such a traumatic time. Your da had just died and I couldn't talk to anyone. I was so angry with the garage because I thought they were careless. And they *were* careless. Your da shouldn't have died trying to do his job that he loved.' Ma paused and I said nothing, just waited for her to go on. 'And Davy worked with your da. He was there the day of the accident when ... when it happened. And he was so angry. Angry with himself and with everyone around him. And – oh my God – so angry with the garage owner. He wouldn't go back working there. He said he couldn't because of the image of your da trapped under the car. Then one night out in a pub he came across the owner of the garage and they had this awful row and Davy struck him with his fist and kicked him and hurt him really badly.'

'But that wasn't in England. How did he get seven years in England?'

'Just listen, Kevin. The guards were called but Davy didn't hang around. He went on the run. At one stage he hid out here but they called and chased him up the stairs and he jumped out the bedroom window and escaped over the back fence. That's when he headed for England. He got a job in a garage and I didn't hear from him for ages. I didn't know where he was living or who he was hanging out with but they must have been a bad bunch. He was always a bit wild so he was bound to get in with the wrong sort, especially since your da wasn't around to keep an eye on him.'

'What happened, Ma? What did he do?'

'Rita rang me and told me he'd been involved in some sort of botched robbery.'

'Botched?'

'Failed.'

'What did they rob?'

'It wasn't really a robbery. It was what they call a tiger kidnapping.'

'They tried to kidnap a tiger?'

Ma laughed and then suddenly she stopped and her face went all serious. 'Oh, Kevin, I'm sorry.'

'Ma, just tell me what happened.'

'A tiger kidnapping is where robbers select someone who is high up in a bank – say, like a manager. And then they find where that person lives and they watch the house – are you all right, Kevin? You're gone pale.'

I nodded even though my stomach felt sick.

'Then they break in at night-time and they keep the family hostage while the bank person has to go into the bank and take whatever money they can get out and bring it back. And when the robbers get the money, they release the hostages.'

'Davy was in prison for that?'

'He was the driver for them.'

'And they got caught?'

'Yeah. From what I read about it, it sounded like they weren't the sharpest knives in the drawer.'

'But why did he get so long?'

'Because they carried guns.'

'Did Davy ... have a gun?'

'He said they made him take one because they had to scare the people in the house. He said his wasn't loaded.'

I got up from the table.

'Where are you going?'

'I don't feel right, Ma.'

'Sit down, Kevin, and talk to me.'

'I don't want to talk about it.' I couldn't talk about it. My stomach felt sick like I was going to puke.

'Sit down, Kevin. Please!'

'I'm going up to my room to watch telly.'

'I'm sorry, Kevin. I don't know why I didn't tell you all this before.'

'You should have told me, Ma. You should have told me sooner.'

'I'm sorry, Kevin. I really am.'

I left the kitchen feeling dizzy and headed straight for my bedroom and sat on the side of the bed.

I remembered how Davy was so interested in the stuff in the black refuse sack, and then him and Adam appearing on Conor's road. I hadn't seen either of them get out of the car. Davy hadn't brought the bag back to Jenny. The only reason they were on the road was to watch Jenny's house. And Conor said he felt like someone was watching him. Someone *was* watching him but it wasn't his own da. It was Davy and Adam who were doing the spying. He must have found info in the bag that showed Jenny was a bank manager and maybe even that her husband had died.

Everything made sense now. I thought of the gun and what they were going to do with it. I looked at my phone to check the time. It was just gone seven o'clock. I tried to think what I should do. Maybe if I told Ma she might know. But she covered too often for Adam and she wouldn't want Davy going back to prison again.

I wanted to call Rory and tell him. But I knew I'd only scare him and he'd want to call the guards straight away or he'd get his da to call them. But maybe they weren't at Conor's house yet. Maybe if I got there ahead of them

170

I could warn Conor and Jenny. I turned on the telly and kept the sound down low and sat on the bed waiting for Ma to come upstairs for her shower.

I didn't have long to wait before I heard her on the stairs. She opened the bedroom door and peeped in.

'Are you OK, Kevin?'

'Yeah, Ma. I'm fine. I'm just watching a movie and then I'll go to bed.'

'OK, Kevin. And tomorrow we can talk some more about it. If you want to that is.'

'OK, Ma.'

As soon as she closed the door, I went straight to my wardrobe and pulled out my sleeping bag and the spare pillow. I pulled back the duvet on the bed. I placed the pillow in the middle of the sheet and the rolled-up sleeping bag above it and then I spread the duvet back over them both so it looked like I was asleep in the bed. I placed the remote at the end of the bed so Ma could turn off the telly like she usually did. I changed out of my clothes and put them on the bed. I got a fresh tracksuit top and jeans from the wardrobe. I quickly put them on and then listened at the door until I heard the noise of the shower from the bathroom. I eased open the door and stood to listen to the splash of water and Ma's happy voice singing her 'Love, love me do' song. I crept down the stairs and took my jacket off a chair in the kitchen and then I headed out the front door.

The white van was gone. I headed for the bus stop to wait for a 75 bus. I stood there for about fifteen minutes and no bus came so I decided that I'd walk and run to Conor's house. In my mind I could see Davy and Adam wearing balaclavas and knocking on Conor's door and Davy with a gun in his hand. I was hoping I was wrong about them. I was hoping that they were really on their way somewhere to shift furniture.

As I moved towards the end of the estate, I passed by Mags and Jake Boylan but I don't think they saw me, cos Mags was on the skateboard and Jake was whingeing at her to get off it. Mags was wobbling like jelly on it, like it was the first time she'd ever been on one. I put up my hoodie and they didn't even notice me passing by cos Jake was laughing at Mags cos she'd fallen on her arse. The pink bike was outside her house, lying against her garden wall. Her red jacket was rolled up and clamped onto the carrier. I stopped now and glanced back towards them. Jake was on the skateboard and moving too fast on it and Mags was shouting at him to stop. They were going in the opposite direction to me, so I knew she'd never notice me taking the bike. I pulled the jacket off and threw it on the garden wall, then hopped up on the bike and pedalled like crazy until I was clear of the road and heading for the short cut through the park and the other estates.

21

Conor's road looked dead, like nobody lived on it. I cycled on the path on the opposite side of the street and eyed the house. There was a white van in the driveway parked right beside the Beemer. It had been reversed in and was blocking the view of the front door. The number plate looked different but there was no mistaking the bird-crap stains on the front of it. It was Davy's van. Davy was inside the house. But was Adam in there?

I cycled up to the top of the road, looking for the entrance to the laneway that led down the back of the house. I found it easy enough, just two houses up from Conor's. There was a rusty gate at the entrance. It was locked with a heavy chain and padlock like you'd see on a motor bike. I gazed down along the lane and I could see it bending in around the back of the houses. There was long grass in the middle, and nettles, docks and other long weeds growing along each side.

I leaned the bike against the gate like I was going to leave it there, but then I worried that someone might come and steal it. I heaved it up until the side of the bike lay on the top bar, but before I could climb up after it to let it down the other side, it slipped from my grasp and clattered into the lane. A dog barked behind one of the houses on the other side of the street. I peered around to see if anyone else had heard the noise but there was nobody stirring at all on the road. The barking stopped. I hopped the gate, lifted the bike and pushed it along the grassy track.

As soon as the lane curved away from the road, I threw the bike down into the ditch and then my eyes scanned the wall. Conor's house was the third door up. I tried to open it but it was locked.

I climbed the wall and, once inside the garden, I headed straight for the shed and hid behind it. Then I stuck my head out and peered towards the house.

I could see the two footballs up on the grassy area near the goalposts. There were clothes now on the line and I could make out the shape of Conor's football gear hanging there.

I sneaked down the garden, a couple of trees at a time, and then I sprinted as far as the trampoline. I scrambled in underneath it and peeped out towards the sun room and the back door. I remembered my phone in my pocket and I grabbed it out and switched it off.

I crawled out from under the trampoline and went round to the side of the decking that was nearest the bar.

I moved quickly up the steps and in behind the lemon curtain to see where Conor had put the key. There was a tiny sink there with a cracked pint glass in it full of scummy water. The tiny counter was dusty with a manky-looking chopping board and a dirty knife lying on it. Two wine glasses hung upside down from a shelf with a spider's web making a bridge between them.

I bent my head beneath the counter to see if I could spot the tin can. I found it easy enough, but as I raised my head I heard the back door slide open. I stood really still and peered through a tiny gap where the two curtains met.

It was Adam. He was wearing some sort of dark blue overalls like workmen use and a balaclava that was pushed up to the top of his head so it looked like a woolly hat. He came to the wooden rail, took out a packet of his cigarettes and lit one up. He stood there blowing smoke until the door slid again and another figure in the same dark blue overalls joined him. I knew it was Davy even before he pulled off his balaclava. He had a mug of tea in his hand and was wearing gloves like a TV surgeon.

'You make sure you pull that back down when you go inside, and leave it down all the time you're here,' Davy said.

'Yeah,' Adam said.

'And where are your gloves?'

'In my pocket,' Adam said and then pulled them out to show Davy he wasn't lying.

'Put them on you.'

'I don't like the feel of them, Davy.'

'Will you put them on you, for Christ's sake. Just as well you weren't a bloody surgeon.'

Adam stuck the cigarette in his mouth and began squeezing his big hands into the tiny gloves.

'And keep them on you. I don't want to get caught just because you've left prints all over the place.'

'I'm putting them on. OK?'

'Give me one of those smokes,' Davy said, and Adam pointed the box at him.

Davy took a cigarette and Adam flicked his Bic lighter at it. It took him three goes before he got it to flame. Then they stood side-by-side looking down the garden.

'You sure there's nobody in the next-door houses?'

'I'm sure,' Adam said. 'One crowd are gone to a wedding down in the bog somewhere and the other lot are away on holidays.'

'That's good.'

'Yeah.'

Neither of them spoke for a minute or two. I was afraid to breathe in case they heard me.

'Where's the gun?' Adam asked.

'Will you stop worrying about it?' Davy snapped.

'I don't know why we can't just send her off for the cash now, and then we could all stay here until she comes back with it.'

'I told you already it can't happen until the morning,' Davy said.

'OK but why do you have to bring the boy somewhere else when she goes to the bank? And why do I have to stay here on my own? Why can't we all stay here together until she comes back with the cash?'

Davy sighed really loud and then he spoke slowly and I could hear menace in his voice that I hadn't heard before.

'Because it's simple psychology. She won't dare try anything smart if she knows the boy won't be here when she gets back and she doesn't know where I've taken him. OK? In the same way she doesn't know now what part of the house we're holding him in. She's up in his bedroom in the middle of all his things and all she's worrying about now is whether he's going to be safe. And in the morning it'll be the same – plus she'll have had all night to fret about it. She'll have worked out that bringing us the money will set her son free; calling the guards will threaten his safety. Do you understand now why it's going to go down the way I've planned? It's a game of strategy like where you have to be one move ahead of your opponent. Well, I'm three steps ahead here. OK?

'Yeah,' Adam said, doubtfully. 'But you'll take the gun with you when you go with the boy.'

'I told you already I would, didn't I? And all *you* have to do is keep your cool and count the cash and call me to let me know how much she's collected. Then you just leave the house and drop the bag with the money in it where I told you. And I'll take it from there.'

'How will I get home?'

'I told you this already as well. You get the bus like it's an ordinary day and you're just going about your business. You'll be at home and I'll be north of the border before anyone even knows what's happened.'

Adam sucked on his cigarette and then blew the smoke like escaping steam down towards his toes. 'I don't want any of it.'

'Any of what?'

'I don't want any of the money. I don't want anything to do with it.'

Davy said nothing, just looked down the garden and blew smoke from between his lips. He tossed the last splash of tea from his mug out onto the grass. 'Now is there anything else that we need to sort?'

'No, Davy.'

'And for Christ's sake don't call me Davy.'

Adam took a last drag on his cigarette and was about to fling it away when Davy stopped his hand.

'What do you think you're doing with that?'

'I'm throwing it away.'

'No you're not. You flush it down the sink or down the toilet. We leave no trace of anything here. Do you hear me? Nothing.'

Adam stubbed the end of the cigarette out on the wooden railing and as soon as Davy turned away from him he flicked the butt off into the grass.

'When are you going to ... move him?'

'First thing in the morning,' Davy said.

'What time?'

'Seven.'

'And what if ...'

'What?'

'What if you're not happy with how much she brings back?'

'Then she doesn't get the kid back.'

'You don't give her back the kid?'

'That's what I've told her.'

'What are you going to do with him? You can't just ...'

'What?'

'You can't just get rid of the kid. And by the way he freaks me out the way he looks like ... you know.'

'I'm not getting rid of him. I won't have to. But we can't have her believing that. As far as she's concerned, she'll never see her kid again if she doesn't get us a decent amount of cash. OK? So she'll get it, and then she'll get the kid. Easy.'

'OK, Davy.'

'I said don't call me that!'

Davy took a last drag from his cigarette and then dumped the butt into the mug. He pointed the mug at Adam.

'Stick your cigarette butt in there.'

Adam stared at the mug.

'What did you do with it?'

'It's in my pocket. I'll flush it when I get in.'

'Jesus!' Davy said, like he was running out of patience.

Davy turned to go back in when a phone pinged. I got a fright cos for a second I thought I hadn't turned mine off. Adam pulled his phone out of his overalls and stared at the screen.

'It's Ma.'

'What does she want?'

'There's a load of missed calls from her. She says she can't find Kevin.'

'What?'

'She says she can't find Kevin. And some girl on the estate said he stole her ma's bike.'

'Show me the phone.'

Adam handed Davy the phone and he stared at the screen.

'Christ almighty, this is all we need.'

He gave the phone back to Adam.

'What will I tell her?'

'You tell her he's here.'

That made me jump when Davy said that. I pulled my eyes away from the curtain and stood frozen.

'Tell her he's here?' Adam croaked. 'But he's not here, Davy. He's missing.'

'Will you do what you're told? Tell her he's with us and we're with a friend of mine moving a bit of furniture. Tell her he'll be back when we get finished but it won't be until tomorrow.'

'Tomorrow!?'

'Yeah, tomorrow! Now go and do it.'

'But, Davy, she's worried about him. I should go and help her to find him.'

'Listen to me. He's not gone far. He's probably off with that little friend of his. Baldy's son.'

'But Davy –'

'Give me the phone.'

I peered through the tiny gap once more and could see Davy take Adam's phone in his hand and then quickly tap in a message. Then he gave the phone back to Adam. 'Now turn the bloody thing off if it's going to be spooking you.'

Adam looked at the phone, then put it in his pocket.

'Listen to me,' Davy said. 'If I didn't say he was here with us, she'd have called the cops – and then they'd be out searching for us as well.'

'OK. But what if something has happened to him?'

'Nothing's happened to him. She's after thinking the worst, like all women. Let it be a lesson for her. She needs to mind him a bit better and not be leaving him on his own all the time. OK?'

'OK,' Adam said, but he didn't sound sure.

Davy turned to go back inside the house. 'Lock that door when you come back in.'

As soon as Davy was inside, Adam took out his phone and then glanced over his shoulder as if to check where Davy had gone. He moved a little closer to where I was hiding and rang a number. He held the phone to his ear but nobody answered him, cos he peered at the phone again and tapped in another number. He glanced over his shoulder once more, and spoke quietly into the phone when it was answered.

'Lizzy! It's me, Adam. Adam, yeah! No, it doesn't matter where I am ... will you just listen. Just listen, will ya!'

Adam was ringing Madser's sister. I suddenly remembered the photo from his room and knew now why he'd kept it.

'Kevin's gone missing and I'm away with Davy so I can't go look for him. We're just away, and I can't get out of it. No, don't call to Ma's house. You'll only upset her cos she thinks he's with me and Davy. Will you just listen! I'm telling you he's not. Jesus, Lizzy, don't ask me any questions. Just ask Mark to go and look for him just in case Cokey Mulligan's done something to him. I know he's a crock, but he has mates. No, Lizzy, no cops if they can't find him. He'll turn up. He's able to mind himself. He's a smart little prick. Yeah. I will, I promise. Yeah, I'll call ya tomorrow.'

He rubbed his eyes with the balaclava, then pushed it back down over his face. He put the phone in his pocket and went quickly into the house. I could hear the door slide and then the click of the lock. It was only then I realised I had been holding my breath for ages and I let out a long sigh of relief.

I turned on my phone and read the messages and missed calls on the screen. They were all from Ma. She had rung six times and left text messages and a long voice message where she sounded like she was crying. She was asking where I was and saying she was sorry she hadn't listened to me when I was upset. I sent her a quick text.

Hi ma cant talk.

with Davy and Adam.

c u 2morro.

turning fone off cos 2 bizy.

Then I did turn it off and stuck it back in my pocket.

I came out from behind the counter and raced up the garden, then stopped halfway up. I turned and went back towards the decking, my eyes lowered to the grass. I found the cigarette butt where the fool had dumped it. I picked it up. The stupid eejit had left it there for someone to find – even after watching hundreds of *CSI* programmes.

I ran as far as the shed. I tried the door but it was locked. I looked across the garden to the long plastic tunnel. I glanced towards the house. There was no sign of movement. I made a dash for the tunnel. It didn't have a lock, just a door made of plastic and wood that had a tiny bolt on it.

Once inside I could feel the heat on my face like it was a sauna. It felt sticky warm. I looked down the length of the tunnel and could see trays and pots with all sorts of plants in them. But the place smelled like everything was rotting instead of growing. In the middle there were tall plants with withered leaves that had stuff like tiny green tomatoes and tiny cucumbers growing from them but the leaves and everything looked sad like bits of burst balloons.

I mashed Adam's cigarette butt in the palm of my hand and then buried it beneath the bone-dry soil in one of the containers. I moved beyond the plants down to the back of the tunnel and saw a clear area that seemed to have just a table in it. I walked towards it and got a surprise when I saw the table wasn't for plants but was a pool table – a real full-sized pool table. There were two cues lying on the green top in among the scatter of balls like someone had gone off in the middle of a game. There was an old black sofa behind the table near the back wall of the tunnel with a small square coffee table beside it. The sofa had a few soft cushions on it and a yellow and blue blanket hanging on the back of it to keep it clean. There was a dirty mug on the table that looked like it had mud at the bottom of it but I knew it was hot chocolate. The table-top was covered in little coffee-stain circles and lots of silver tracks left behind by snails like they were using it as a station.

I sat on the sofa and stared at the pool table and at all the plants that were thirsting for water. Nothing would happen until seven o'clock, Davy said. I wasn't sure what I was going to do but I knew I had to get into the house before seven to see if I could get Conor and Jenny out without Davy and Adam noticing. I had a few hours to kill so I took out my phone and switched it back on but silent. I placed the cushions at the end of the sofa and I lay down on it and pulled the blanket around me. The place was so warm, I felt like I wouldn't need the cover but I knew it would get cooler as the night came on.

I wasn't sure if I was going to be able to sleep cos it was an awful lot earlier than I'd normally go to bed. I closed my eyes and tried to think of nothing but it was impossible, cos all my thoughts crowded and crackled in my head like they were the bumper cars at the fairground.

I started thinking about Ma telling me about Da's accident and now I could see a clear picture of Da's garage and the huge door is wide open and I can see Da trapped under the car he's trying to fix. His face is twisted with pain and he's crying out and Davy is suddenly there and he's trying to lift the car off him like he's Superman. But he's not Superman and then there's all these other guys there jacking up the car and Davy has Da in his arms and Da's roaring out like he's a wild animal. I open my eyes cos I can't bear to watch any more. I try to think about something else but when I close my eyes this time I hear Conor's voice saying the tunnel is boring and I can see the look of sadness in his eyes and now I know exactly where his da died. I open my eyes to banish the thought cos it's scary but as soon as I close them again I get a sudden memory from when I was very small. I'm in the church in the very front row. The church is crowded and everyone is sad and I'm sitting on Adam's lap and he's squeezing me too tight and his head is so close to mine that he gets my face all wet with his crying. And I wipe his cheek with my fingers and I tell him big boys don't cry.

I blink my eyes open again and feel even more scared, cos I want to go home. But I know I can't. I have to save everyone in the house, not just Conor and Jenny, but I don't know how I'm going to do it. My thoughts keep racing and I think of Sully and wonder why I didn't tell him about the gun and maybe if I had then none of this would have happened. I see a picture of him with his arm around Ma's shoulder and then I hear his voice and he's explaining all the rules of chess to us and I can hear the groan he makes whenever we beat him cos he's not that great at chess at all even though he thinks he is.

Then I think of Adam when he was good fun to play with, and us watching telly together. Him making loads of popcorn in Ma's huge glass bowl and the two of us fisting it into our mouths like our hands were diggers. I think of Ma and I can see her worried face as she fingers Da's earring and then suddenly I remember that's what I used to do when I was very small and tired and he was holding me in his arms. I open my eyes but I can't keep them open. The heat in the place makes me sleepy. I let my eyes close.

22

I'm on a skateboard and Davy and Adam are on a pink bike that Adam has stolen. Adam is pedalling like crazy and Davy is sitting behind him on the carrier smoking a cigarette and with a cup of tea in his hand and he's telling Adam to be careful cos he's spilling some of his tea. I'm chasing after them but I can't keep up with them.

Then I'm sitting on the stairs and there's smoke coming from the sitting room and when I look in I see it's not smoke it's steam cos Ma has the iron out and she's ironing Sully's shirt with the black buttons and he's sitting on the settee with no shirt on and watching *Friends*. Then I hear Rory at the front door and he's saying we've to go up to the hills and track the trail left by Cokey Mulligan, cos he wants to find the spot where he got beaten up and maybe there'll be blood and we can collect cigarette butts like in *CSI* and we'll be able to identify the guys that did it and banish them to another planet. But I don't want to go with him cos he wants to bring Mags Boylan with us. Instead I sneak into Rory's back garden and I'm sitting in this huge jacuzzi that his da has gotten installed and I get a fright cos Mags Boylan is suddenly there with me and I'm not sure what she's wearing or if she's wearing anything at all and she starts laughing and the water starts to get lovely and warm and Mags says, 'Is it just me or is this starting to get very hot?' And I jerk suddenly awake in a cold sweat.

When I grab the phone I see I've only been asleep for a couple of hours. It's dark outside and the inside of the tunnel is gloomy and spooky with plant shadows. It feels cooler too. I pull the blanket tight around me and lie back down on the sofa and close my eyes again, this time trying not to think about anything at all.

23

I felt a hand on my shoulder and a gentle squeeze to let me know it was my turn to pot the ball ...

I shot up on the couch and peered towards the pool table and then along the tunnel, just to make sure there wasn't anyone there. I closed my eyes and tried to remember the dream. Conor and his da had been playing pool and I had to play the winner. Or maybe it was my own da that was playing. It was like the dream flew off somewhere before I could remember it properly. I opened my eyes, relieved to see the two pool cues hadn't been moved. I didn't want to spend any more time with these dark ghostly shadows.

I peered at the phone, it said 5.30. I turned it off and put it in my pocket. I moved to the door of the tunnel and inspected the back of the house. There was nothing stirring and hardly a breeze.

Everything was so peaceful I found it hard to believe that Conor and Jenny were being kept hostage inside.

I walked quickly down the garden and headed for the little bar. I got in behind it and took the key from the tin can. I leaned in low to get a look through the glass door but nothing moved on the other side of it. I put the key in the lock and twisted it, then very slowly and carefully slid the door open just enough for me to fit through. Once inside, I eased the door shut and locked it with the key. I stood and listened for movement but heard nothing. I stepped silently past the doors to the sun room and the wet room and made my way into the scullery. The door to the kitchen was open. I stood and leaned my head in.

I could see Adam sprawled asleep on the couch. The black balaclava made him look like a weird sort of ragdoll that had been thrown aside. One of his hands was on his belly and the other was hanging down towards the chess board floor. His box of smokes and four empty beer cans were on the floor near that hand, and an empty naggin of something that looked like gin or vodka lying on its side. There was a large half-empty bottle of 7Up sticking out of a black kitbag he had taken from his bedroom.

I leaned my head in further and I saw Conor sitting asleep on an office chair that wasn't there the last time I'd been in the room. I got a fright when I saw him cos he had a black hood over his head which had a piece cut out for his mouth. His head was slumped on his chest and the hood looked like a balaclava they had put on backwards. His wrists were tied to each arm of the chair by black cable-ties that you'd see electricians use. Ties! *Ties* – not *toys*. These were the ties that Davy and Adam had been talking about. I felt like a stupid eejit.

I stepped into the room, my eyes searching for something to cut the plastic with. I had no plan except to get Conor out and then I'd search and see if I could find Jenny and maybe release her as well. I looked towards the worktop and spotted the knives in the knife block. I went over and took out the smallest one. Beside the block there were four of the black cable-ties still in a plastic ziplock bag. I stared at them and suddenly a different plan, a better plan, came into my head. I turned to look at Conor and thought about how Rory said me and Conor looked so alike, and then I remembered how his jersey fit me perfectly the times I had tried it on. Now he was wearing a blue hoodie that was zipped up, with pockets like pouches at the front. He wore the same jeans he had on that day at the carnival as well as the same Nike runners. I glanced down at what I was wearing, then stepped quickly to his chair and put my head really close to his.

'Conor,' I whispered as loudly as I dared.

I glanced at Adam but he was away with the fairies.

'Conor! Conor!'

He jerked suddenly awake.

'Shh! Don't say a word. It's me, Kevin.'

His arms moved like he was trying to raise them, but then he must have remembered where he was because he went completely still. I lifted up the hood and he gaped at me with his big wide terrified eyes.

'Kevin!'

I put a finger to my lips and nodded to where Adam was in case he'd forgotten. Then he saw the knife in my hand and his head jerked back.

'It's OK. I'm just going to cut those cable-ties off you.'

He nodded, and I quickly sliced through the plastic. He lifted his arms and massaged each wrist but he didn't move from the chair. He looked dazed like maybe he wasn't sure if he was coming out of a dream or going into one.

'Kevin?'

'Yeah, it's me.'

He stared out towards the garden and then towards Adam as if he was replaying something in his head. His eyes widened and his mouth fell open.

'Are you ... are you an ...'

'Yeah, an angel, now just shut up and do what I tell you and you'll be able to get out of here safe.'

He gazed up at me but showed no sign of moving out of the chair.

'Come on,' I whispered and tugged gently on his sleeve.

'Come on,' I said again and let his sleeve go and headed back towards the scullery door. I turned and beckoned for him to follow. He glanced towards Adam and rose slowly off the chair. He staggered and nearly fell. He held onto the side of the table and waited for a few seconds and then he came quietly towards me. I headed into the scullery and turned to wait for him.

'They have my mum tied up in my bedroom. I'm not leaving without her,' he said, his eyes watering with tears.

'I know,' I said. 'I know she's there.'

I looked at his jeans and hoodie. We were definitely the same size. The only difference was the backs of his hands were more tanned than mine and didn't have any scratches on them, but there was nothing I could do about that. I took off my tracksuit top and handed it to him. He stared at it.

'What are you doing?'

'Listen to me, Conor. I'm taking your place and moving you out of danger.'

Conor frowned like it was too much to think about.

'We're swapping places. OK? So you have to tie me in the chair and then go and hide in that small room like when you played sardines with your da.'

Conor's eyes moved towards the door to the little store room.

'Yeah, in there, until you hear the man taking me away. That means your mother will be on her way to the bank. Can you do that?'

His eyes moved back to me and he nodded but looked unsure.

'This is what your da wants you to do. OK?'

'My dad?'

'Yes! So when that happens, you go out the back door.'

I took the key out of my pocket and handed it to him. 'Here's the key.'

He stared at it dumbly and then up into my face like I was a magician or something.

'Take it,' I said, and pushed the key into his hand. 'You can't leave until your mother goes and the man takes me away in the van. Do you understand, Conor? Once you hear us driving off, then you can make a run for it. Or use your bike if you can. It's at the side of the house. You go and find your mother at the bank and she'll ring the guards when she knows you're safe.'

'How will you get away?' Conor said, his eyes wide with worry.

'When he sees I'm not you he'll have to let me go. He'll know the whole thing is botched. Now swap clothes.'

'I'm scared,' Conor said.

'Do you remember the carnival?' I said.

Conor frowned.

'Remember the Freak Out – how scared you were before you got on and then you were able to manage because it wasn't as scary as you thought it would be. Well, you can manage this too. OK?'

He nodded and started to take off his hoodie and then his T-shirt. Quickly we got out of our clothes and started swapping them. It was almost funny but it wasn't funny at all. I emptied my pockets but all I had was the key to my house and some loose change and the photo of Adam and me with Santa Claus. Conor had nothing in his jeans except for some gum, and all that was in the pockets of his hoodie was scrunched-up paper hankies. I stuck my phone beneath all the tissue and hoped it wouldn't be noticed. Then we swapped runners. His felt tight like he had smaller feet than me but I just squeezed up my toes and said nothing.

When we were ready I poked my head in the door to make sure Adam was still out of it. He was. I crept towards him and the box of smokes that lay on the floor. There was just the one cigarette left in it. I took out the photo from my back pocket and slipped it into the box.

'Hey!' Conor whispered at me from the doorway. I turned and nodded at him and then I went to get the plastic bag with the ties in it and took two out. I sat on the chair and handed one of the ties to Conor.

I looped the other one round the arm of the chair and made a wide noose. I placed my hand inside the noose and tightened it until I could hardly even twist my wrist.

'Quick! Do the other one,' I said. Conor copied what I'd done and pulled the noose, but left it way too loose. 'You have to pull it tighter,' I said. He stared at the black tie and then did what I asked.

'Did ... did Dad ... really send you?'

'Yeah!' I said. 'He sent me. And he's watching now and he'll be pissed off if you mess it up. Now go – go and be a sardine.'

A strange smile came to Conor's face and all the fear went from his eyes. He turned to look one last time at

Adam and I knew he wasn't afraid of him any more. Then he headed for the door.

I was relieved that we had managed to get this far without Adam wakening or Davy hearing us. But Conor stopped in the doorway like he was about to change his mind once more. I felt like shouting at him to go. But he just stopped and turned around. He pointed at my head. I made the word 'WHAT' with my mouth. I couldn't believe that he was changing his mind and was going to ruin everything. He came quickly towards me and bent down to pick something up from underneath the chair. It was the hood.

'For feck's sake,' I said.

He didn't speak a word but pulled the hood gently around my head and then down until everything went black. He rested his hand on my shoulder and pressed it gently. I got a shock cos it was the exact same spot that the hand in my dream had pressed.

I didn't even hear him leave. I listened to my own breath as it settled and then to Adam's twisting movements and groans. I let my head fall back against the back of the chair not sure if I'd be able to sleep.

24

The alarm startled me as soon as it sounded. It was beeping from somewhere out in the hallway and for a second I thought it was Ma's. I tried to move my arms and when I couldn't I realised where I was. I waited for Adam to waken but his breathing didn't change. I could hear sounds from upstairs like Davy was moving about. A toilet flushed. A door opened and then the sound of a voice coming down the stairs that was soft but afraid. I couldn't hear what was being said, only mumbling. Then I heard footsteps out in the hall and the voices getting louder. I could hear Jenny's voice like she was pleading, like she was asking to see Conor, but I didn't hear what Davy said in reply. The voices faded once more and the front door opened. There was silence for a few seconds until I heard Jenny's car being started. The front door clicked shut and the footsteps came back down the hall towards the kitchen. I let my head slump forward on my chest to pretend I was still sleeping.

Davy muttered a curse, and his feet moved quickly across the tiled floor towards the sofa. He must have poked Adam with his fingers cos Adam woke with a start and sounded like he didn't know where he was and grumbled about being woken so early.

'I told you not to touch any booze,' Davy hissed at him.

'I couldn't sleep, could I?'

'You didn't have to drink everything in the house.'

'I didn't drink everything in the house. I just had a few beers.'

'From a gin bottle,' Davy said, annoyed.

'I'm fine, OK?'

'You don't look fine. You look like you've been dragged backwards through a hedge.'

'Don't do my head in. I'm fine. I'm awake.'

'You'd better be fine. I don't want you messing this up on me.'

An empty can rattled on the floor and a glass bottle slid in my direction and hit the leg of the table. Adam cursed.

'Just clean it all up and put everything in the black refuse sack I left out for you. And here – take this.'

'I'm not taking that! You said I didn't have to.'

'I've changed my mind, cos look at the state of you. She might even think about clocking you instead of handing over the cash.'

'I don't want it,' Adam said.

'You listen to me,' Davy said, getting narked. 'You'll take it and when she comes in the door, you wave it in front of

198

her face so she stays terrified. And she's not going to stay terrified if she thinks there's only one gun and I've gone away with it.'

'But Davy –'

'Will you shut up calling me that?'

'He's asleep.'

'OK! Now here, take the gun and show her you mean business like I said.'

'What if it goes off?'

'It can't go off because there's no bullets in it.'

There was silence like Adam was staring at the gun and thinking about his next move.

'And what am I supposed to do with it when I'm finished?'

'Put it in the bag with the money and leave it where I said.'

There was silence again.

'Can you manage to do that much?'

Davy didn't wait for Adam to answer. 'Now when you've collected your rubbish go and get a knife and cut the boy loose.'

I started to panic when I heard that cos I couldn't remember where I'd left the knife or the cable-ties I'd cut off Conor. Had they fallen to the floor or had I brought them outside when we were changing? Davy moved away and I could hear Adam collecting his empty cans. Then his steps moved off towards the counter as he went in search of the cable ties. I waited for him to call Davy but that didn't happen. There was silence and I wasn't sure where either of them was. Then I could sense Adam standing right beside me. His hand was on my hood like he was going to remove it. I jerked my head to the side, like to show I was awake now.

'What the hell are you doing?' It was Davy's voice cutting the silence and Davy's steps coming quickly towards us.

'His hands are different,' Adam said, his voice shaking.

'What?'

'Look! See! His hands. They're different ... they're like ...'

'What? Like what?'

'Nothing! I'm just saying ...'

'Are you on something?'

'I'm not on anything. I'm just saying his hands look different, that's all.'

'And what about his runners? Are they different?'

'No.'

'And his jeans and hoodie? They haven't changed colour or anything over night? Or what about the balaclava on his head? Maybe that was a tea-cosy yesterday.'

'Stop! I'm just saying, OK?'

'What are you saying?'

'We shouldn't be here. We shouldn't be doing this.'

'We are here. We're doing this and I need the money even if you don't. Do you hear that? And I can't do it without you. OK? Now cut those ties off him and when you take him out to the van take your rubbish along with you.'

Davy moved away and Adam leaned close to me. I felt the back of the blade cold on my skin as the knife cut through the plastic. I didn't raise either hand, just let them lie on the sides of the chair. Adam must have gone to collect the bag of rubbish cos it was Davy's voice now that was in my ear.

'Listen, kid. Me and you are going for a little drive in my van. Nod your head if you understand that?'

I nodded.

'Good. Now, we're going to lead you out to the front of the house and you'll get in the back of the van and then we're going to tie your wrists to the spare wheel. Yeah?'

I nodded really fast, to let them know I'd be no trouble.

'Good lad. You do what you're told and you'll see your ma in a couple of hours. Try any funny stuff and there's no telling what'll happen to her or to you. Are we clear on that?'

I nodded once more.

'Get two of those ties you brought,' Davy said to Adam. I could hear Adam going to the sink to search for them.

'There's only three left,' he said.

'That's OK. You just need two of them.'

'But I need two ... for the woman.'

'For Christ's sake, I thought you said you brought plenty.'

'I thought I did. I must have dropped some of them.'

'Will you just take two of them and look for the ones you dropped when I'm gone.'

'OK, OK!'

'Use one of them to tie his two wrists together and use the other to tie him to the wheel. Do you think you can manage that much without screwing it up?'

Adam didn't answer. Davy moved away towards the scullery and I hoped Conor wouldn't make noise, or panic and try to make a run for it.

I listened out for more sounds but Adam suddenly took hold of my arm and nudged me out of the chair. I pretended to stagger and he paused like he was waiting for me to get my balance. Then he gripped me by one wrist and brought the back of my other wrist up against it and tied my crossed hands together with a cable tie. I could feel his own hands shake as he tested the connection.

'That's not too tight, is it?' he said.

I shook my head.

'This will be over soon so don't fall down now,' he said as if to himself as well as to me.

He moved me along beside him and when we got to the door I could feel the cool air on my arms. Once outside he steered me ahead of him and when we got to the door of the van we stopped. He dropped the bag of rubbish onto the gravel and I could hear the keys rattle and the van door creak open. He took my hand and placed it on the van floor to show me how far I had to step up. I lifted my leg and he placed my runner on the edge of the floor.

'Hey, they're my socks.'

I stopped and turned my head towards his voice.

'I mean ... Christ. Just get in will ya.'

I felt his hands on my elbow and then the light push of his fingers and I leaned into the back of the van and he guided me forward till I was completely inside and fell on something that I knew immediately was a bean bag. I heard the rattle of tin cans and a clink of glass as he threw in the rubbish bag and followed quickly after it. He pushed the bag aside and took hold of the cable tie that was around my wrists and raised my arms up towards my face. I held my arms in that position and I could feel him loop in the other cable tie and then he pulled on it gently and my arms moved higher and the backs of my hands brushed against the spare wheel.

'Listen to me,' Adam's voice whispered in my ear like he was going to tell me a secret. 'I'm leaving the cable tie loose so you can slip out of it first chance you get and make a run for it. Do you hear me?'

I nodded my head again.

'Thanks, Adam,' I said.

There was silence. Then his shocked voice. 'What did you say?'

I could feel his hand on the balaclava ready to whip it off my head.

'What are you doing?' Davy's voice was at the door of the van and Adam's hand fell away.

'I – I was just talking to him ... telling him he'll be OK.'

'Christ's sake, it's not a crèche we're running. Now go back inside.'

I could hear Adam scramble out of the van, then the sound of Davy taking his place and swearing loudly. My wrist got gripped and the cable tie shortened as the backs of my hands pressed against the wheel's inner circle of steel.

I groaned to let him know it was sore but he said nothing.

'I thought I told you to go inside,' I heard him hiss at Adam as soon as he was back out of the van. 'Christ's sake, just go in! And remember. You won't have too long to wait. You tie her up and you leave with the money and for God's sake don't walk down the road with your balaclava still on.'

'I'm not an eejit.'

'Well, then stop acting like one.'

I could hear Adam's feet on the gravel as he headed for the door. Then he stopped.

'I'm not sure I can do this,' I heard him say like he was close to tears.

'Well, it's too late to back out now. So just go inside.'

'But ...'

'What?'

'I don't want to do it. He ... he could be Kev ... and she ... she could be Ma.'

'GO INSIDE NOW!' Davy banged the van door shut, giving me a fright.

Then I could hear him going round to the driver's door and climbing in. The engine started and the van moved off, crunching on the stones and then smoothly over the cobblelock as it headed for the road. I sat with my head against the tyre and pressed the side of my body into the beanbag like I was making a nest. I thought of Conor and hoped he had used the key while we were all outside and was waiting now, maybe at the side of the house, ready to race off on his bike to catch up with his ma and let her know he was safe.

The van travelled only for something like ten minutes or so and then it stopped and the engine was cut. There was silence. I couldn't believe that Davy had parked already. I thought he had planned to drive for ages. I heard the handbrake being pulled. The radio came on and he switched channels a couple of times and then switched it off again. I heard him light up a cigarette and the window gliding open.

Somewhere in the distance I thought I heard a sound like I'd heard that day at the carnival. It was like the sound of a generator. It *was* the sound of a generator! I knew now where Davy had parked and was waiting for Adam to bring the money. Suddenly I remembered Davy hugging the man with the grey ponytail. The man must have given him the van. Maybe they had been in prison together and Davy had done something for him and was having the favour returned. It was perfect – like, who'd notice a white van parked in among all the other vans and trailers at the carnival site? That meant Davy's car must have been parked there as well cos there had been no sign of it at Conor's house.

'He's not going to come,' I said.

There was silence. The window slid back up.

'What did you say?'

'Adam. He's not going to come with the money.'

'What the hell –'

The driver's door of the van suddenly opened and banged shut. After a couple of seconds the back door opened and I could hear Davy climb in beside me.

'What the hell are you saying?'

'Adam. He won't come with the money. He's a dickhead.'

The hood got pulled off my head, nearly taking my two ears with it.

'Hiya, Davy,' I said, looking him straight in the face.

Davy couldn't speak, he got such a fright. His eyes widened and his mouth opened like he'd just seen a ghost. He backed away from me as though he was afraid.

'It's just me, Davy. Kevin.'

He stared at me and his mouth moved but no words came out. Then his hand went to his forehead and he slumped back against the side of the van.

'What the hell? How – where the hell did you – Kevin, what the hell are you after doing?'

'No, Davy, what are you after doing?' I shouted. 'You promised Ma! You promised her you'd bring all the stuff back. I heard you talking and all that crap about your hands being clean. And they're not clean cos you didn't bring it back. You didn't. Instead you spied on them and you end up trying to rob them.'

'I'm not robbing them! I'm robbing a bloody bank.'

'No you're not, Davy. You're getting her to rob it for you.'

'Just shut up, will you. If everyone does what they're told to do then nobody gets hurt.'

I could see the anger flash in Davy's eyes but I wasn't going to let it stop me saying what I wanted to say, especially cos my own anger was rising up inside me like boiling milk in a saucepan.

'What do you mean, Davy? What kind of hurt are ya talking about? Like, how are they ever going to be normal again? How? How are they ever going to open their door to anyone again? How are they going to do that? And how are they going to stay living in their house that's already filled with enough sad memories to last them for ever? Answer me that, Davy? How? And they have names, Davy. Conor and Jenny. That's who they are. And Conor's da died suddenly like my da died and you know what that was like cos you were there.'

'ALL RIGHT!' Davy shouted like he couldn't bear to hear me talking to him.

'And you were supposed to take Da's place in the house. I wanted you to take Da's place. And so did Adam. And you were supposed to keep Adam out of trouble. That's what Ma wanted from you. That's how you should have been able to please her. Keep Adam out of trouble – not do something to land him in jail.'

'I said all right! OK? Now shut up and let me think.'

He rubbed his face with his two hands then thumped the back of the driver's seat like he was trying to break it. Then suddenly he let his body slump against the side of the van and he groaned really loud like he was going to cry.

'Davy, there's nothing to think about. It's over. Conor is on his way to warn his ma, so she's not going to come anywhere near the house. She'll go straight to the guards. And even if Jenny comes back with a suitcase of money, Adam's not going to be there to take it off her. He's too scared of that gun and you should never have involved him in the first place. Like, what would Da say to you, Davy? And what are we supposed to tell Ma? What kind of lies will she have to make up for all of us if the guards find their way to her door?'

Davy whacked the side of the van with his fist. 'You're a little fool, Kevin. Do you know that?'

He pulled a small knife from his pocket and stared at the blade. Then he got to his feet and bent his body towards me with the knife out in front of him. I remembered the story Lunchbox told me about what Davy did to Cokey Mulligan and I pulled away from the blade and pressed myself up against the spare wheel.

'Ah, for Christ's sake, what do you take me for?' he said as he held my wrist and placed the blade under the cable tie and cut it in two.

'Get out of here now and go home,' he said, like all the fight had been taken out of him.

I stared at him and didn't move. I rubbed at my wrist and then brushed past him and out the door of the van. Once outside, I looked around at where we were and I saw

I was right cos it was where the vans that belonged to the carnival were parked. Davy's car was parked next to the white van. I waited for a minute or two but there was no sign of him getting out of his seat. I wondered what he was going to do and it was like he was just sitting in the van, like a beaten chess player hopelessly staring and trying to find a move that wasn't there.

Then the door of the van suddenly opened and Davy jumped out and slammed it shut behind him. He didn't even look towards where I stood but made for his car and unlocked the boot. He had Adam's black bag of rubbish in one hand, and a canvas bag in the other that must have held his balaclava and overalls. He seemed ready to fling both bags into the boot but then he paused and looked about him and his gaze rested on two nearby large metal wheelie bins. One of the bins had bursting bags of rubbish pushing the lid open but the other bin's lid was closed. Davy strode across to the second bin, lifted the lid and peered in. Then he opened Adam's rubbish bag and stuffed his own canvas bag inside and knotted the top of it. He tossed the binbag inside and then took three manky looking bags from the other bin and threw those in on top of his own rubbish. He banged the lid shut and strode back to his car and got into the driver's seat. He started the engine and I moved out of the way so he could see properly where he was reversing. When he had backed out far enough, he opened the window and stared at me. I gazed back at him.

'See ya, Davy,' I said, even though I wasn't sure if I'd ever see him again. The car moved forward over the worn grass and towards the road. Then it stopped with the engine humming. I waited for it to move again but it didn't. I walked slowly up as far as it and peered in the open window at Davy in the driver's seat. He was staring forward towards the road. Then he turned towards me and smiled his crooked smile.

'You're a clever little prick, aren't you?'

'Yeah, Davy,' I said.

'I should have had you in my gang and not the other fella.'

'I don't want to be in anyone's gang.'

Davy shook his head like there was nothing else he could think to say.

'I didn't want you going back to prison, Davy. I didn't. That's why I did what I did. And Adam didn't want you going back to prison either. That's the only reason he came with you even though he was terrified. So I don't care if you're angry with me for messing up your plan. I don't care cos I don't want you going back inside. And I know you were angry with Ma cos she wouldn't let you live with us full time, and maybe that's why you did what you did. But she likes Sully. I don't know why but that's just the way it is.'

'OK! OK!' Davy said like he'd heard enough out of me. He stared out through the windscreen like he was caught between two minds, like maybe he was thinking there was still a slim chance that Adam would turn up with the money.

'Maybe I should wait for Adam to get clear and I'll give the two of you a lift home.'

'No!' I said, louder than I meant to say. 'No way, Davy! There's just no way you can ever come near the house again. You have to go way up north like you planned.' I could hear Sully's voice talking about banishment and my eyes suddenly filled with tears. 'It's botched, Davy. You botched everything for everyone and what's Ma going to say when she hears what you did?'

'You're going to tell her?' Davy said and I could see the look of fear in his eyes.

'I dunno – but I think I'll have to. She needs to know cos what's she supposed to say if the guards do turn up at her door and wanting to know where we all were. I don't want to tell her, Davy, cos I know she'll be ashamed of all of us. She'll have to lie to try and protect us. But I don't want her having to tell lies any more. And I don't know if she'll be able to lie for you after what you've just done. So you've got to go away, Davy. And stay away.'

Davy said nothing, just rubbed at his face with his two hands.

'You have somewhere to go, don't you?'

Davy sighed like he was suddenly really tired.

'These people here, they need a mechanic so I'll go up north and wait for them there.'

'That's good,' I said, capturing tears with the back of my hand that were crawling down both cheeks.

'Yeah,' he said.

'Goodbye, Davy,' I said.

He turned his head and his eyes looked sad like maybe it had suddenly dawned on him that everything really was botched up.

'Yeah,' he sighed and turned his head away. Then the window slid up and the car moved off. He waited until another car let him out into traffic and I watched him disappear from sight and out of our lives.

I cleaned out my eyes with the fingers of both hands and stood there watching more cars go by and thinking about Conor. Davy would have taken his phone and Jenny's also but I knew he was well on his way to meet her, and as soon as she saw him she would know he was safe and they needn't be terrified any more. In my mind I could see him and Jenny running towards each other and her hugging him like she hugged me that day I wanted to hand over the kitbag. I could see her examining him from head to toe to make sure he was all right, and then she'd hug him again.

I felt bad that they had to be terrified like that, and it was my fault for having taken all that stuff from the robbed car in the first place. I felt sad too that I'd never see Davy again and it really was like he was banished. And it was me that had banished him. But banishment was better than the thought of him cooped up in prison like a goldfish in a bowl with bigger fish snapping at his tail and only making him meaner than when he got put in there.

I rang Adam's number but there was no answer. I texted him a message. Then I headed for the bus stop home, hoping I'd find him already there waiting for me like he was one of those pawns that made it to the end line and could be exchanged for a better piece. I was listening out for the sound of sirens but there were only the ordinary morning traffic noises of people hurrying to work.

There was no sign of Adam at the bus stop. Maybe he hadn't figured out what was going on cos he hadn't smoked the last cigarette yet. I waited five minutes and the bus loomed into sight and pulled into the stop and the doors hissed open but I didn't get on. The driver shouted out something narky in my direction and then the doors hissed once more and the bus was gone. I checked my phone and rang Adam's number once more and sent him another text when he didn't answer my call.

I was just about to run back towards Conor's house when I saw a cyclist pedalling like crazy onto the roundabout and heading in my direction. It was Adam. And when he came closer, I could see where he had got the bike. It was pink and he looked some sight on it with his long legs working furiously and his black kitbag dangling from one shoulder. He whizzed past me and I shouted his name and the brakes squealed and he came to a sudden stop. He turned his head and when he saw me his face broke out in a beam of a smile.

'Feck's sake, Kevin, will you come on, ya mad yoke. Anyone sees me on this pink contraption and I'm history.'

'The gun, Adam. Where's the gun?' I shouted as I ran towards him, suddenly afraid in case he was bringing it back to our house.

'I dumped it.'

'Where?'

'I gave it back to Davy. It's in the black bag with all the other rubbish. And that's the place for it. What the hell happened there, Kevin? What the hell?'

'You stopped being a dickhead, that's what happened,' I said. I jumped on the carrier and he turned and gave me a smile with his eyes that reminded me of Da. Then he turned around to the road ahead and I held onto the back of his jacket as he got ready to wind up the pedals and take the two of us home.

EPILOGUE

It's three weeks since everything happened. I've leaned Rory's bike against a tree and I'm poking the chain with a twig like I'm cleaning the greasy mud off it but my eyes are glued to what's happening just down the road. There's a SOLD sign in Conor's front garden. A removal lorry has driven away, but Jenny's Beemer is still parked outside the front door.

It's three weeks since everything happened. Three weeks but it feels like forever.

Me and Adam decided not to tell Ma the truth about where we really were that night or what went on in Conor's house. Adam told her that Davy decided to stay up north cos he wanted away from Deegan and he got the offer of a job but had to start straight away. Ma was full of awkward questions, but so relieved and happy to see us that she didn't push us on any of our answers.

Then for a whole day after, all we seemed to do was watch the news, eyes glued to the telly, and listening out for talk about a botched tiger kidnapping. But there was nothing about it anywhere. Nothing! Not a word. Adam wouldn't leave the house but didn't like being trapped in it either just waiting for the guards to call to the door. I couldn't bear hanging round so I headed down to the Spar and checked all the papers. But there was no mention at all in any of them about what happened to Jenny and Conor.

We couldn't understand it. It was like it never happened. But it did happen. I told Adam all about how I met Conor and Jenny and about the football match and about Conor's phone and how I returned the football gear so it looked like it fell from heaven. And I explained how I changed places with Conor and how his da had died suddenly out in the tunnel.

When I told him the whole story he said Jenny mustn't have gone to the guards about the kidnapping. He said it was the only answer that made sense. She must have decided that Conor had been through enough without having to be dragged in front of cameras and talking about an angel and having his photo splashed on the front page of all the newspapers. And it makes sense what Adam said cos I know Jenny wouldn't want Conor exposed to more upset.

I went back to school but I'm not able to concentrate on anything and I want to tell Rory what happened but I know I can't cos I'm ashamed of what Davy and Adam did and I'm afraid Rory might leak it to his da. And I'm ashamed of my part in it too. I want to tell Becky and maybe she'd be good to tell, cos I know she'd keep it to herself. And I want to tell Ma but I know I can't do it yet.

Nobody has heard from Davy. Rita called to the house and spent her time whispering to Ma and when I asked what was going on Ma said they were just chatting about stuff and it needn't concern me. But I know they were talking about Davy and maybe wondering why he disappeared so quickly off up north. And maybe Davy has told Rita something or made up a different story about why he left. But if Rita knew something she'd tell Ma cos they tell each other everything.

Adam didn't leave the house for a whole week after it happened. He spent most of it in his room and only came down when Ma called him for food. I heard him once or twice on his phone talking quietly to Lizzy but he spoke so low I wasn't sure whether he was breaking up with her or she with him. But then she called for him and he went off out with her for a couple of hours. And when he came back he was in better form and telling Ma about his plan to do some course that Lizzy had told him about.

Sully called one night to tell me the chess was ready to start up again. Ma brought him into the kitchen and then nearly fainted on the spot when Adam made a pot of tea without even being asked. I heard Ma tell Rita on the phone that she can't believe it's the same Adam and maybe Davy did have a good effect on him after all.

But Ma doesn't know what's going on inside Adam's head, or about the two nights he's come into my room to tell me about his nightmare. He says it's the same one each night and it scares the hell out of him. He's in the house watching the telly and the doorbell rings and when he goes out to answer it he sees Jenny and Conor and they don't say anything to him. They just stare at him with empty zombie eyes and they hand him a black binbag that rattles with his empties. And he runs indoors and hides in his room. But the doorbell rings a second time and this time when Ma answers it he hears the voice of Cokey Mulligan outside and when Ma comes back into the kitchen she has a wheelchair and she's all upset cos she doesn't know why she's been given it.

The door to Jenny's house opens and I forget all about Adam's dream. An oldish looking man with glasses and wavy grey hair comes out. He heads for Jenny's car and gets into the driver's seat. He reverses the car and turns it so it's facing the road. He beeps the horn then gets out and stands at the car door waiting.

Conor appears first and goes to the car and turns to gaze back at the house. Jenny appears next and Conor and the man watch as she stares back into her hallway before slowly closing the door. Then she turns towards Conor and she pauses and they wait for her to walk towards them. Then all three of them turn to face the house and the man puts his arm around Jenny and pulls her close to him and she rests her free hand on Conor's shoulder. Then the man gets into the car and Jenny goes to Conor and hugs him tight and he lets her. They separate and Jenny gets into the front of the car and Conor disappears into the back. The car moves slowly over the gravel and the cobblelock towards the road. Suddenly it stops and the back door opens and Conor climbs out. He looks back at the house then up into the grey clouds that cover the sky. He has something in his hand which is yellow and he walks to one of the trees with the silvery white bark and its leaves thinning now like Sully's hair. He disappears behind the tree and now I'm not sure what he's doing. When he comes back into sight there's nothing in his hand and he gazes up into the sky once more before he dips back inside the car.

The car rolls slowly onto the road and moves away into the distance with its indicator light blinking, and disappears around the corner.

I wait for a few minutes then drop the twig and wheel the bike along the path until I'm across the road from Conor's house. I lean the bike against a wall and walk over, keeping my eyes on the tree. I see the jersey where he has left it dangling on the branches. It's the goalie jersey I wore for the match, I'm sure of it. I turn it around and hold it up but then I'm suddenly aware I shouldn't be here and someone will think I'm stealing it. But I know it's been left for me. A gentle breeze blows the leaves and I hold the jersey to my chest and look towards the sky and I think of Da and Conor's da and I want to get home to Ma and show the jersey to Adam so he'll know that Conor and his ma are going to be OK.

Acknowledgements

They say it takes a village to raise a child. It feels like it took a village to complete this book and I owe a great debt of gratitude to all of you who have helped me on this journey.

Thanks to Siobhán Parkinson, Matthew Parkinson-Bennett and Gráinne Clear at Little Island for believing in this story. I really appreciate all your sound advice, your brilliant editing skills and your attention to detail.

Thanks to my old friends in F-Troupe who trusted me to write for them all those years ago. Thank you to everyone associated with St Anne's N.S. Fettercairn, Tallaght (inspiring teachers, dedicated parents and wonderful pupils) for the impact you have had on me as a person and a writer. Thanks to Kathryn Coffey of Stage 51 for your constant encouragement and to all those teenagers I've had the pleasure of writing for.

Thank you to my Barnstorming Writing Group who have given me such great writing support and friendship down through the years – John A. Connolly, Kymberly Dunne-Fleming, Lucinda Jacob and Trisha McKinney.

I appreciate also the input of the facilitators on the MPhil Programme in Trinity College: Gerald Dawe, Paula Meehan, Deirdre Madden, Julian Gough and Siobhán

Parkinson. It was in that creative environment that this story came to life. Thank you also to Jonathan Williams for your strong words of encouragement having read that first completed draft.

A huge debt of gratitude is due to The Wilde Things, who offered amazing support and friendship and provided such thoughtful feedback on the early chapters of the book. Tierney Acott, Mary Ballingham, Claire Brankin, Karisa Cernera, Aisling Ettarh, Niamh Griffin, Siobhán Hegarty, Kate Kavanagh, Nina Logue, Mary Catherine Murray, Eamonn O'Reilly, Fiona O'Rourke, Bryce O'Tierney and Shane Tuohy. Special thanks to Fiona, Niamh, Siobhán, Tierney and Shane for the time and attention you gave to a much later draft.

A big thanks to my family and friends who have always supported me and who continue to be an essential part of the village.

Éile and Maebh, you are a constant source of joy and inspiration.

And last but not least a huge thank you to Gráinne, the love of my life, for your belief in me, and for insisting on asking those awkward questions!

14/9/19

ABOUT THE AUTHOR

James Butler's background is in education and drama. He holds an MPhil in Creative Writing from Trinity College Dublin. For many years he taught in a school in Tallaght, setting up a theatre group who went on to write plays performed in the Civic Theatre. In 2005 his first play for children, *Stuck in the Mud*, was nominated for an Irish Times Theatre Award. In 2011 his play for teenagers *The Teen Commandments* was included in the Trinity College London Anthology of Award Winning Plays. In 2016 his radio play *The Carpet Clown* was produced by RTÉ Drama On One as part of The PJ O'Connor Awards. His latest play, *Scattered*, explores the transition made by children from primary school to secondary, and was performed in Clonmel in 2018.

ABOUT LITTLE ISLAND

Based in Dublin, Little Island Books has been publishing books for children and teenagers since 2010. It is Ireland's only English-language publisher that publishes exclusively for young people. Little Island specialises in publishing new Irish writers and illustrators, and also has a commitment to publishing books in translation.

www.littleisland.ie

Little
Island